Lunch with Lenin

and Other Stories

Deborah Ellis

Lunch with Lenin

and Other Stories

Fitzhenry & Whiteside

Text copyright © 2008 by Deborah Ellis

Published in Canada by Fitzhenry & Whiteside,
195 Allstate Parkway, Markham, Ontario L3R 4T8

Published in the United States by Fitzhenry & Whiteside,
311 Washington Street, Brighton, Massachusetts 02135

www.fitzhenry.ca godwit@fitzhenry.ca

10 9 8 7 6 5 4 3 2

Library and Archives Canada Cataloguing in Publication

Ellis, Deborah, 1960-
      Lunch with Lenin and other stories / Deborah Ellis.
ISBN 978-1-55455-105-7
I. Title.
PS8559.L5494L85 2008   jC813'.54   C2008-902324-2

**U.S. Publisher Cataloging-in-Publication Data
(Library of Congress Standards)**

Ellis, Deborah
Lunch with Lenin and other stories / Deborah Ellis
[184] p. : cm.
Summary: A collection of short stories that explore the lives of teenagers affected directly or indirectly by drugs.
ISBN: 978-1-55455-105-7 (pbk.)
1. Teenagers — Substance use – Juvenile fiction. 2. Teenagers – Drug addition – Juvenile fiction. 3. Short stories, Canadian.
I. Title.
[Fic] dc22   PZ7.E4557Lun 2008

Fitzhenry & Whiteside acknowledges with thanks the Canada Council for the Arts, and the Ontario Arts Council for their support of our publishing program. We acknowledge the financial support of the Government of Canada through the Book Publishing Industry Development Program (BPIDP) for our publishing activities.

Canada Council   Conseil des Arts   ONTARIO ARTS COUNCIL
for the Arts   du Canada   CONSEIL DES ARTS DE L'ONTARIO

ANCIENT FOREST™
FRIENDLY

Preserving our environment
Fitzhenry & Whiteside chose to print the pages of this book on recycled paper and saved these resources[1]:

energy	water	greenhouse gases	solid waste
13 million BTUs	70,768 L	1,761 kg	515 kg

41 trees were saved for our forests

Printed by **Webcom Inc.** on Legacy Hi-Bulk Natural 100% post-consumer waste.

[1]Estimates were made using the Environmental Defense Paper Calculator.

FSC
Mixed Sources
Product group from well-managed forests, controlled sources and recycled wood or fiber
Cert no. SW-COC-002358
www.fsc.org
© 1996 Forest Stewardship Council

Cover image courtesy of Pascal Milelli
Design by Kong Njo

Printed in Canada

To those who struggle
to make their way

࿚

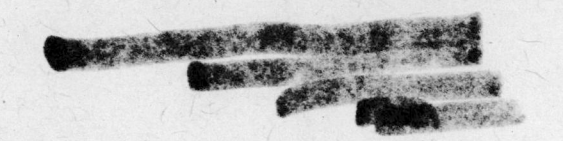

From the cactus villages in Bolivia, the riverside in Manila, to the boot camp in New York, these stories reflect the lives of people I've met and have been able to learn from. I give my thanks to them, and I also thank my editor, Ann Featherstone, for making the stories readable.

Contents

Through the Woods

Matthew tugged his shirtsleeve down to cover the bruises. He worked hard at not looking conspicuous. He didn't want to draw any attention.

He took one last glance in the mirror before leaving the boys' bathroom. Tidy, short hair, cargo pants and nondescript shirt, open face. He looked too young for fourteen, but it worked to his advantage on days like this. No one would notice him. No one would guess.

The kids who looked the part were like the ones at the other end of the row of sinks. Guys in denim over layers of t-shirts, streaks of blue and orange in their hair, bits of metal gleaming from their ears, eyebrows, and noses. Guys who would bad-mouth a teacher even if they were being complimented. Guys like that were always suspect.

But Matthew never was. He got good grades, returned his library books on time, paid attention in class, and spoke respectfully to teachers. Not too respectfully. That would make him stand out. They'd wonder, *Who is this kid who's always so polite? What's he up to?* Nobody did that with Matthew. He was the sort of kid an adult would look at and, in a fraction of a second, decide, *He's all right. No need to bother about him*, and move on to someone who looked like trouble.

"Take a picture, moron," one of the metal boys said, catching Matthew looking at them. They knocked him into the sinks as they left the bathroom. Not hard, just the usual sort of random male violence that high school was all about. Usually, the thugs left him alone, just like the teachers did. It was no fun messing with someone who didn't look scared. Instead, Matthew looked like someone who would fight back, hard, if he was really pushed enough. He would, too. That was something else his open, boy-face camouflaged. He wasn't afraid of pain. Not anymore.

Matthew picked up his books from the floor where they'd fallen and went out into the jungle of the corridor. Eat or be eaten. There was always something to avoid. Sneering groups of girls he didn't like. Jenna, a girl he did like, clinging as usual to the school's sports hero, Cro-Magnon Guy. Athletes throwing basketballs in the hallway—forbidden, of course, but that was how it went. And teachers, those unpredictable creatures with the powers to ruin his whole day. Matthew would have tried to blend in even if he wasn't on a mission.

Today's date with destiny was waiting for him in the library. The Religious Studies shelf was positioned in such a way that anyone standing there had a clear view of the library door and the study hall, where bored teachers prowled, looking for trouble. The librarians behind the desk couldn't see what was happening in Religious Studies. No one went to that shelf except for the sci-fi freaks, looking for books on UFOs. And they'd stay away once they saw that Hammer was there.

Matthew entered the library and saw the hulking figure of the football captain waiting for him. Hammer looked almost comical, pretending to browse the shelf. Matthew didn't go straight to him, but approached in a circular way, through Biology, Biography, and back behind History.

"Searching for God?" Matthew asked Hammer in a voice just above a whisper.

"You're late."

Matthew checked his watch. He was early but he didn't say so. They were there to do business, not to argue.

He took down a book on liberation theology. Peasants and workers overthrowing tyrants around the world. It was his usual choice. The size was big enough for cover, and the title was interesting enough to be plausible. What kid wouldn't dream of overthrowing tyrants?

Matthew always thought up elaborate schemes for this moment. Should he pretend to sneeze and reach into his pocket for a handkerchief? Should they count to three, then do the exchange? But once he was there, though, quick and simple always seemed best; and it was always over with before he had a chance to get theatrical about it.

He had a single fifty-dollar bill folded small and tucked into the side pocket of his Chinos. Matthew assumed Hammer was overcharging him, but what was he going to do about it? He held the book open in one hand, and with the other, he handed over the money. Hammer gave him a small, plastic ziplock bag. Almost as quickly, Matthew made it disappear. On business days he always wore his cargo pants. The bag in his pocket wouldn't be noticed.

"How nice to see you in the library, Alexander." Mr. Hennessy, one of those soft-soled teachers, suddenly appeared beside them.

Hammer stumbled and fumbled. Matthew quickly picked up the ball.

"He asked me to help him find a prayer for the

locker room," Matthew said, keeping his voice calm and polite, even though his insides were shaking, rattling, and rolling.

"Big game coming up against Brant Collegiate," Hammer said, recovering. "Wouldn't hurt to have an edge."

"There's another edge that will help you," Mr. Hennessy said. "It's called studying. Big test coming up, too." Mr. Hennessy taught Geography.

"I could give it a try," Hammer said, with a grin. Football stars could make jokes with the teachers.

Then two girls in the study hall started arguing about sharing space at one of the tables, and Mr. Hennessy went off to lay down the law.

"Great," said Hammer. "What if he talks to the coach? What am I supposed to say?"

Matthew reached up and pulled down a book called *Prayers for All Occasions*. "Your coach will be impressed," he said and started to walk away.

Hammer grabbed his arm. "What about some meth?" he asked. "I can get you a good price."

Matthew pulled his arm away and left the library. Business was over.

There was still the afternoon to get through. Matthew was always tempted at this point to keep the plastic bag on him, close to him, but it was too big of a risk. Suppose it fell out of his pocket? Every now and then, police would walk through the school with drug-sniffing dogs. The students had all been warned. Announcements were made regularly that this could happen, and notes were sent home with each report card. Dogs would find the bag in his pocket. Matthew hoped his locker was safe.

The lunch-time corridor was crazy with activity. Couples necking, kids arguing, boys harassing girls, girls harassing girls. The air stank of old lunches and desperate survival.

Matthew got to his locker. He looked around without appearing to look. Then it was just a matter of leaning the right way and making a quick transfer. He'd already positioned his gym shoes. The plastic bag fit right down inside the toe. Right after it, he shoved in his bunched up, still-damp gym socks. He'd worked out especially hard in gym class that morning. He hoped that, if this was a dog day, all the dog would smell at his locker was stale foot sweat. It wasn't a great plan, but it was the best he had so far.

Three classes in the afternoon: Physics, Math, and Biology. Fortunately, they were the sort of classes that required concentration. Matthew could get lost in formulas and equations, only occasionally losing his focus to the bag in his gym shoes. History or Literature classes gave him too much time to think.

At the end of the day, he had to stop and chat with his teacher about the Math Olympiad coming up. That was normal, and everything normal had to be done. Putting his shoes and socks in his backpack afterward was normal, too. Anybody would do that.

Still, he felt like he had a big sign over his head as he left the school and headed through the town—a big, Las Vegas neon sign, flashing on and off. Arrest This Boy.

"Hello, Mrs. Pierce," he said to a friend of his mother's, who was stepping out of the Clip and Curl. Mr. Dreyer, the owner of the hardware store, lived next door, so Matthew had to greet him too as the man straightened the collection of lawn rakes leaning against the store wall.

It's a normal day, Matthew thought. *I'm heading home from school on a normal day.*

When he got through the downtown, he didn't turn right when he passed the cenotaph, the way home.

He turned left instead. He crossed the High Level Bridge, high up over the Grand River. But he paid no attention to the view. Views were for the way home, when the job was all done.

At the store on the corner he bought a couple of Kit Kat bars and a pack of rolling papers. It wasn't far now. The Meadowvale Nursing Home was just ahead.

"Hello, Matthew." The nurse on duty at the front desk greeted him with a smile, the same as always. "She's out by the fountain."

"Can I take her for a little walk?"

"I think she'd like that. Don't let her get chilled, though."

It was a warm day, but getting chilled on warm days was an old-lady specialty.

The little woman in the wheelchair sitting by the fishpond had pain written on her face, but it brightened when Matthew walked into the sunroom.

"I'm always so afraid for you," she said as he bent down to kiss her cheek.

"Couldn't be easier," he said. "Ready?"

She already had her shawl draped across her lap. He put it around her shoulders to keep the nurses happy. They left by the front door.

Gran was so slight it wasn't hard work at all to push the wheelchair up the hill, along the little dirt pathway behind the Home, through the woods, all the way up to the old Anglican cemetery. The groundskeepers had just given the lawn the final mow of the season. The grass was short and it was easy to roll the chair to the bench under the maple tree. The leaves on the tree were so brilliantly red they looked like they were on fire.

Matthew opened his backpack and took the little plastic bag out of his gym shoe.

"How are things at home?" Gran asked.

"The same," he said, then corrected himself. "Better." He tugged on his shirt cuff.

Matthew did the rolling. Gran's fingers, once nimble and intelligent, were too arthritic now for such fine work. He passed the joint to his grandmother and struck a match.

"I wish I could have kept you with me," she said.

"It's better now," he told her. "Really." He motioned for her to put the joint in her mouth, and he touched the flame to it.

She took a long breath in, held in the smoke, then exhaled slowly, with relief. She smiled at Matthew.

"Nothing else works," she said. She filled her lungs again with the drug. Matthew had told her how to smoke it, passing on what Hammer had told him. "Pretty professional for a lifelong nonsmoker, eh?" she said. She said that every time.

"Top of the line," he told her.

Matthew settled back on the bench and rolled the rest of the joints while Gran smoked. He felt her relax beside him, the pain and the tension sliding away.

The rolled joints made a little pile on the bench. Later, they'd have fun hiding them around her room for her to smoke on her own when he couldn't be with her.

The last joint he rolled made a small, smooth tube, a little slip of a thing he could cup in his hand and drop into his pocket. He could smoke it later, leaning over the railing of the High Level Bridge, looking down over the river and waiting for the night to fall and his parents to pass out. Time and pain would disappear with the smoke, and for a while, like Gran, he would be at ease and at peace. He ran his fingers over the joint, smoothing out the wrinkles, imagining what it would feel like to have that weight and worry lifted off him.

"Kit Kat?" asked Gran. She grinned.

Matthew grinned back. He put the joint on the little pile with the others, and broke out the Kit Kats. They ate the chocolate, Matthew getting Gran to eat half of his along with hers—she was so thin!—and they looked out across the graveyard at the changing colors of the trees. They listened to the birds and exchanged small thoughts, and Matthew doubted that he'd ever feel this close to anyone, ever again.

Pretty Flowers

She stood in the middle of her family's poppy field, giving Zameer a lesson. The sky was a clear, brilliant blue—as blue, Tahmina thought, as her own eyes and those of her younger brother's as well.

"You can't cut too deeply," she told Zameer. "Just cut the skin. If you cut right into the pod, the *sheera* will pour out too fast, all over the ground. And how will we collect it then?"

Tahmina was an expert. She'd harvested opium with her father for two years on another family's plot, and she knew, just knew, how much pressure to put on her knife. It was good to be good at things. Tahmina was twelve years old, and good at five things: harvesting opium, arithmetic, planting things so that they would grow, looking after her little brothers, and making her mother laugh.

Their poppy field was prettier when the flowers were in bloom. All pink and white or purple. It wasn't so pretty now that the petals had dropped off and blown away, although the round heads on top of the tall, slender stems were beautiful in their own way. Tahmina liked the way they bobbed in the wind.

"Let me try." Zameer balanced on his crutch and reached for the small, sharp knife in Tahmina's hand.

"No!" Tahmina moved the knife out of Zameer's reach. "You know what Papa said. Get it perfect on an orange first. Opium is money. We can't afford to have you ruining money."

"Oranges are money, too, for that matter," Zameer said. Zameer had a logical mind. He wasn't always right, but he defended himself well. "They cost money to buy, and if we grew them, we could sell them the same way we sell our opium."

"But the oranges are still useful to us, even if you butcher them," Tahmina said. "Watch closely, now."

She took hold of the green seed pod and made a couple of cuts around it with a knife—not too deep, just right. A white, milky sap began to ooze out from the cuts, nice and slow.

"That will turn brown in the sun. Tomorrow morning, we'll scrape it off and spread it out to dry."

"I'll help with that," said Zameer.

"You'll have to ask Papa."

"I already did, and he said yes."

Tahmina didn't like sharing this chore. Of course it was right that Zameer would work. Everybody in the family worked, except the youngest. But couldn't Zameer do something else?

Being with their father inside the low mud walls surrounding their little poppy field was her special treat, something she got in exchange for being the oldest. Sometimes, when the harvest looked good, the baby was well, and they all had enough food, Papa would reach far back in his memories, to kite-flying tournaments, family feasts at holidays, and pomegranates in his family's orchard. "Bigger than your head," he would say, putting his hands on Tahmina's head as if to measure it and see if it would make a good pomegranate.

Tahmina had never seen the family's orchard. It had belonged to Papa's father, and his father, and his father, and his father. Papa claimed that Alexander the Great once dined on his family's peaches and figs and pistachios. The orchard had stood up to the centuries of droughts, floods, and locusts. Then one day a plane dropped its bombs, which turned the land to fire, eating up all the trees.

Papa and his family had gone to a refugee camp in Pakistan. And when the camp was bulldozed, the

United Nations Refugee people had taken them to a little plot of land in Helmand Province.

"We'll start a new orchard," Papa had said when he first saw the plot. But the land was too rocky for fruit trees, and the climate was too dry for cotton. They managed a little plot of wheat, and kept a few goats and chickens. They had a bit of bread, a bit of milk, a few eggs. For everything else, there was opium.

Tahmina worked quickly. Their field wasn't big, but it held a lot of plants, and she wanted to be all done by the time Papa got back from the village. Zameer got tired of watching and went down and sat on the low wall. He wouldn't admit it, but Tahmina knew his leg was bothering him. A landmine had blown off one leg and hurt the other one in a way that had never really healed right.

"Maybe, when the crop is in, we can buy him some medicine," Tahmina said to herself. She felt rich, and so it was easy to also feel generous.

Most of the money would go to pay back Mr. Najibullah, the local shop owner who had loaned them the money for seeds, food, and other things they needed over the winter while their crops grew. But they would have the seeds from this year's poppies to plant next year's crop, and that would save them money. There wouldn't be a lot extra, and Tahmina probably wouldn't get any of it for pocket money; but she might, and it was fun to plan out what she would do with it.

A school uniform, maybe, although it wasn't necessary for the school she went to, two days a week. More notebooks and pens, maybe even a book to read. Or she might just tuck the money away. Ramadan was coming up; for the celebration of *Eid al-Fitr*, she could buy presents for everyone in her family. A new cap for Papa, bracelets for her mother, a ball for her brothers. Spending money in her head helped her work faster.

Mama came out of their small mud hut and sat on the wall, holding baby Aryan in her arms. Tahmina's other brother, Zmarai, who was younger than Zameer, stopped his game of tossing stones in the circle target on the ground and joined the others. They didn't talk, just sat in the sun. Tahmina felt good, working while they watched, like she was doing something important, something that would help all of them.

Tahmina heard a motor running but didn't bother turning around. It was probably just a tank. They often drove by, sometimes a long line of them, from the foreigners' military base a few miles away. They drove in one direction, and a little while later there would be the sound of explosions in the hills. Then they'd drive back the other way, all dusty, with the soldiers looking tired and sometimes bloody. Sometimes her brothers got excited; they'd wave and run alongside the tanks— well, Zameer couldn't really run, but he could hobble quickly. If the explosions had gone well and the soldiers were happy, they might toss a sweet or two down to the boys.

Tahmina never joined in. She was too old, and a girl, so she had to act with more dignity. Her brothers usually shared with her. At least Zameer did. Zmarai was still at the stage where he'd gobble up whatever he could get.

As the rumbling got closer, it didn't sound like a tank any more. Tahmina looked up from her poppy slashing. A police van followed by two bulldozers entered the yard. Everything stopped in front of their house.

"Tahmina!" Mama called, pulling her burka down over her face. These strange men coming uninvited into the yard did not have the right to look at her.

Tahmina came out of the poppy field. She and Zameer walked up to the men. Zameer would do the talking, since he was the oldest boy. Tahmina would be right behind him, to give him courage.

"*Salaam alaykum*," Zameer said, with a slight bow, to show respect.

"*Salaam*," the man in charge said. He wore a police uniform. Dark glasses made it impossible for Tahmina to see his eyes.

"Where is your father?" the man asked.

"He is in the village," Zameer said. "May we offer you some tea?"

"I will speak with your mother, then."

"My father will return soon," said Zameer, looking puzzled. Who was this Afghan, so ignorant of manners?

"It's about your poppy fields," the man in the dark glasses said. "It is illegal to grow opium. You are breaking the law."

"My father will return soon," Zameer said again, glancing back at his sister. Surely now the man got the point?

"Everyone has been warned. I'm sure I'm not telling you anything new. It's against the law to grow poppies. The president has declared it, and I am here to enforce it."

"My father—"

"I know, your father will be back soon. How do I know this is true? How do I know you even have a father? Maybe he was killed. My own father was killed. It happens. You think I don't know what it's like? You have mouths here to feed. I know this. I have a family, too."

Tahmina stared at the bulldozers, realization and horror filling her.

"I've been ordered to destroy the poppy crops. There are too many heroin addicts in Europe, so I must destroy your poppies. It's not me. I don't want to do this. I am also Afghan. I know how it is. But there are addicts in Paris, addicts in Rome. I must destroy your poppies. Those are my orders."

"No!" Tahmina yelled, even though it wasn't dignified or modest. But maybe, for this, yelling could be forgiven. "My father had to borrow money for us to live. It must be paid back in opium. Leave us our poppies this time. We won't plant any more. I promise." She had no right to make such a vow, but a terrible fear was growing in her. "Our debt..."

Her mother rushed forward and began to argue with the officer as well.

"I have my orders," the policeman kept repeating.

Mama, with the baby, Zameer, Zmarai, and Tahmina linked arms and stood at the entrance to their field, the one Papa used when he brought in the hand plow to dig furrows into the hard ground.

"We will not let you do this!" Mama said firmly, making her voice loud even though her face was covered. "We have nothing to do with the choices of Europeans or anyone else. We are farmers. We will not let you do this!"

The bulldozers kept coming. They drove right past Tahmina's little family. The powerful steel machines drove right through the mud walls as if they had been made of fog. They tore up the poppy plants, then

rolled their big wheels over them, mashing and grind-
ing into the ground all the money Tahmina had pretended to spend. They trampled any hopes the family
had to live without debt, to build a new future, to start
again after so many, many failed efforts.

All around the field the bulldozers plowed—
digging up, running over—until not a single stock
stood and not a single pod was unmashed. The whole
crop bled its money into the poor, rocky soil.

The machines drove back out through another
wall, as if they were still hungry to smash things, then
came to a rest back out on the road. Two men with
masks over their faces and canisters in their hands
got out of the van and sprayed foul-smelling stuff
all over the broken crops. Tahmina's hopes of at least
collecting the seeds were dashed. The poison would
kill everything.

"You were warned," the policeman said. "I did not
want to do this. I have a family. I have mouths to feed,
and you were warned." He slammed the door as he got
back into his vehicle.

The van and the bulldozers went on down the road.
Tahmina's family was too stunned to even cry. They
sat on the broken wall, breathing in the stench of the
poison. They were still sitting there when Papa
returned from the village.

When their father saw what had been done to his crop, he turned around and went back to the village to speak to the man who had loaned the family money. He returned that evening with a long and heavy face.

෴

"It's the only solution," Papa said to Mama late that night. Tahmina lay quietly on the *toshak* she shared with Zmarai and listened.

"It isn't," said Mama. "It can't be."

"Find me another way," pleaded Papa. "You think I want this?"

"But there is a future now. The new government has promised. It's not like before."

"We must eat to have a future. We must be alive to have a future."

"But…"

Tahmina wanted to hear more, but Zmarai chose that moment to moan in his sleep. Her parents did not speak again that night.

In the morning, over weak tea and naan left over from supper, Papa said to Tahmina, "You will come with me into the village this morning. We will see about the repayment of the debt."

"I'm going, too," said Zameer.

"No, you are not."

"Yes, I am."

"You will do as you are told," Papa answered.

"I am a man!" Zameer said in his little pipsqueak voice. "I have a right to be included in talks about the family."

Papa stopped arguing. They left right after breakfast. The village was only a mile away, but that was far for Zameer on his bad leg.

Their village had a police station and a small grocery shop that sold rice, soap, and packaged goods from foreign countries. There was also a teahouse where men played chess and backgammon, a kebab place, and a few fruit and vegetable sellers. Papa led them into the grocers.

Mr. Najibullah, the owner, was sitting in his chair in the middle of the little shop. It was a special chair. It could spin and face any direction. When he sat in it, he could turn and watch all the customers, no matter who they were, and make sure they did not steal from him. Whenever Tahmina went into the shop, she always felt his eyes on her, even though she would never think of stealing anything. The chair creaked as he turned in it—he was a big man and the chair springs were tired from holding him up. He had a big scar on his big face from fighting the Russians. Tahmina kept her eyes down as they entered the shop so she wouldn't have to look at the ugliness of his old wound.

"Is *this* the daughter?" Mr. Najibullah asked. "You said she was pretty."

"Tahmina is beautiful," Papa said, putting his hand on her shoulder. Tahmina could feel it trembling.

"You have a father's blindness. How are her teeth?" Mr. Najibullah asked. "I had a wife with bad teeth. Crabby woman, morning, noon, and night."

"Her teeth, like her bones, are strong. She is smart, too. She is good at figures and can help you in your shop."

"Probably has nimble fingers, too, and a good appetite. She won't get anywhere near my shop. Show me her teeth."

Papa gave Tahmina a nudge. Tahmina looked up at him, not understanding. "Open your mouth," he said, gently, sadly. Tahmina opened her mouth. Mr. Najibullah brought his face closer to hers so he could see better. His breath was foul. It was like the poison that spread over their precious poppies.

And then she understood.

"You don't want *her*," Zameer said, suddenly, stepping in between his sister and the shopkeeper. "She's ugly and stupid, and she has a terrible temper. She will make a horrible wife."

"Zameer!" said their father.

"Take me instead," Zameer said.

Mr. Najibullah's eyes widened, then he roared with laughter. "You? What would I want with a broken little boy like you? I have real sons, proper sons. Sons with legs."

"Please excuse my son," Papa said. "He is my eldest boy, and I have not taught him silence as I should have."

"Your boy is a delight, but you may keep him. Your daughter will do. She is not as valuable as opium, but she can help my other wives with their duties and give me more sons. We will have the marriage soon, so that you do not have time to smuggle her out of the district. Some men actually think they can avoid paying their debt that way. There is no honor left in Afghanistan when men skip out on their debts. Tell your boy to take her outside while we complete our business."

Zameer and Tahmina went out onto the dusty street. Tahmina was having a hard time breathing.

Zameer took her to a bench outside the shop and helped her sit down. She put her head down and tried to control herself.

"Run away," Zameer said.

Tahmina raised her head and took a gulp of air. "What?"

"Run away," Zameer said again.

"I can't," she said. "The debt."

"Run away, and the old goat will have to be content with me. It will be easier for me. You can't do this."

Tahmina looked down the long dirt road that disappeared into the Afghan dust. She looked at her little brother; then she stood up and staggered to the corner of the building where she was violently sick to her stomach.

The walk back home was long and slow. Papa held tightly to her hand and cried with every step.

Tahmina didn't cry. She thought about the poppies, broken and in the ground. She thought about the journeys she had taken with her family. She thought about her mother, strong and smart, and her father and brothers—all of them brave.

Across the plains, in the hills, explosions rumbled. Dirt shot high up into the air. It swirled around and settled on the fields and the people.

And the fine, soft powder settled over all the pretty flowers.

The Dark Side of Nixon

Brandon opened her purse. She never gave him enough. She counted out every nickel. "This is what your milk will cost," and she put it into a little envelope marked *Milk*. "This is what your lunch will cost," and she put it into a little envelope marked *Lunch*. Usually she made his lunch, but now that he was in high school, she sometimes let him buy it. But she always seemed to know how much a school lunch would cost, and there was never anything extra.

He needed money for other things, but she would never believe him.

"You don't have to pay to use the school bathroom," she'd said, as if she knew, as if she went to school every day. "You've got to learn to stand up for yourself."

Stand up for yourself but don't fight. Speak up for yourself but don't shout. You can do it, but there's no shame in failure.

All his life, nothing making sense. Nothing working properly.

Stupid, all his life.

He was smart about finding his mother's purse, though. She kept hiding it, and he kept finding it. She'd yell that she was going to call the police on him, but she never did.

This time, her purse was right out on her bed, asking him to open it. He couldn't see any bills, but he grabbed whatever coins he could hold in his hand.

This time, he found something else. A small plastic chip that read "Five years."

He went down to the kitchen. Mom was finishing the supper dishes.

"Mom, what's this? I found it in your purse."

His mom turned around, dripping soap suds. "In my purse? How many times have I told you?"

"It says *five years*." He held the little disk up to her. "What is it?"

Mom turned back around. "They give those out at AA. It means I haven't had a drink in five years."

Brandon didn't understand. "A drink?"

Mom left the casserole dish in the sink to soak away

the remains of the scalloped potatoes. "You remember when I used to drink—beer and wine and gin. You remember."

Brandon never paid much attention to what his mother did.

"I guess it's time we talked about this. I stopped drinking over five years ago, and Alcoholics Anonymous gave me that little disk to remind me of my achievement." She dried her hands on a dish towel, sat down at the kitchen table, and pulled a chair out for Brandon to sit with her. "I'd still be drinking if it weren't for you."

"I did something good?"

"Do you remember back in grade five, before your dad left, how we took you to all those doctors?"

"Uh huh." He didn't, really. But if he was in the middle of doing something good, he didn't want to argue.

"We couldn't figure out what was wrong with you. All those tantrums. All those problems in school. You seemed smart, but you could barely add two and two."

Brandon knew he was no good at arithmetic. He didn't need to be reminded of that.

"Wipe that scowl off your face. I'm not going to nag you. The doctors told us you have FAS."

Brandon sounded it out. "F-A-S. Fas?"

"Fetal Alcohol Syndrome. I was drinking a lot when I was pregnant with you; because of that, you have this condition. After they told me, I decided to stop drinking. I went to my first AA meeting that evening, and I haven't had a drop of alcohol since."

Brandon couldn't grasp it. "My problems are your fault?"

"It's not like I set out to make your life difficult. I just didn't know any better. I was just a kid myself when I had you, not much older than you are now. I wasn't a very bright kid, either."

She kept on talking, but Brandon had stopped listening. He was hearing other things in his head— teachers yelling at him for fidgeting in his chair, classmates calling him "retard" and "stupid," kids laughing as they grabbed at his homework full of blotches and mistakes.

And then he heard her say, "I learned that you need structure and clear instructions, and that you are quite capable of doing many things. A lot of people have it much worse. I hope you're not going to start using this as an excuse."

"It's because of *you* that I'm like this?" That's when Brandon knew he had to go or he'd have to start throwing things.

"It's because of me that you're here at all, so watch your tone!"

"You think you did me a favor by having me? You didn't do me a favor!"

That's when he left without sitting first on the step to put on his shoes, messing up his whole routine. And now he was in his bedroom slippers and without his jacket.

Brandon walked, fast-furious. Sometimes even that pace was too slow, and he broke into a run until he got out of breath and had to slow to a walk again.

Not that there was anywhere to walk to. Some roads went east and west, some went north and south, and some ended up in fields with broken-down tobacco barns.

Brandon wasn't supposed to be out by himself, especially at night, when it was even easier to get lost. But he didn't care. He couldn't stay inside, not tonight, not after all that, because he'd end up throwing things. And he'd worked so long and hard at *not* throwing things anymore. So, he walked. Hard and fast.

Moving quickly kept him warm. Without his jacket, the late September evening was cool.

But tonight, he was too mad to care that he hadn't sat on the step to put on his shoes, and he hadn't reached up to the hook to get his jacket, and he'd left the house in his bedroom slippers.

Her fault. All her fault.

Brandon got to the main intersection of Nixon, where Nixon Road met Wyndham Road. There were no stores or streetlights, like in Simcoe or Delhi or Tillsonburg. There was just a stop sign, and the old Nixon Public School—his old school. And it was just ahead.

It was only one story, only one hallway, small and cozy, easy to find his way around, although it had seemed big at the time. It was closed now. His class was the last one to graduate from there.

Brandon went around the back, where everything was dark and quiet. Cars wouldn't see him back there. If his mom came looking for him, she wouldn't find him.

Bad things had happened to him at this school. Teachers had yelled at him, kids had laughed at him and beaten him. Brandon picked up a rock and threw it at the school, wishing the windows weren't boarded up so he could break the glass. But it was probably a good thing anyway; he'd gotten into trouble breaking the windows before, when he was eight.

With every stone he threw, Brandon remembered something else that made him want to throw more stones. Kids not liking him, teachers not liking him. Sitting forever on that chair outside the principal's office until he couldn't stand it and had to scream and run around, which landed him more time in the chair. Punishments, detentions, kids making fun. Fumbling the ball in the simplest games, always being a few beats behind everyone else.

Her fault. All her fault.

"Who's throwing rocks? Who's in our space?"

Brandon froze. He knew that voice. It was Dwayne. The dreaded Dwayne.

"Death to whoever it is," said a girl, followed by the sound of giggling.

Four of them came around the corner toward the dark side of the school. Dwayne, Sylvie, Sherry, and Nate. He'd gone to school with them. The boys would just beat him up and then leave him alone. But the girls were worse. They rarely said anything to him; it was all done with looks and whispers and giggles.

"Is that Brandon? Look, everybody. It's our good friend, Brandon."

"We miss you at school, Brandon. Why didn't you sign up for Delhi like the rest of us?"

His mother had called them "the Four Horrors." When she'd found out they were all going to Delhi District, she had enrolled him in Simcoe Composite. "A new start," she'd said. He was glad to be away from them, but it wasn't a new start. It was the same old start, except that he kept getting lost at the high school.

The Four Horrors joined him in throwing stones. They weren't very good. They were all sort of falling over themselves and laughing a lot.

Brandon's feet were getting wet in his slippers. He wanted to leave, but he couldn't concentrate on where else he should go.

"You know what I think? I think Brandon thinks we don't like him," Nate said. "Is that what you think, Brandon?"

"No," said Brandon.

"We should have been nicer to Brandon," Sylvie said, putting her arm around Brandon's waist. "Do you have a girlfriend, Brandon?"

"Sure," he said. "Lots."

"Do you? Is there a special one?"

"Joanne," he said. There was a Joanne in his history class. She spoke up a lot, and Mr. Horton was always saying, "Well done, Joanne. You're right."

"Joanne is a nice name," Sylvie said, making her fingers do little curly motions in his hair. "Is she pretty?"

Mostly, he saw the back of Joanne's head, since she sat in front of him. "She has nice hair," he said. "She's really good at history."

"Are you putting the moves on my girl?" Dwayne asked, laughing.

"No!" Brandon showed his hands. "See? No moves."

"Good. Because if you did, I'd have to pound you again. I've pounded you a lot, haven't I, Brandon?" He pulled Sylvie away and started necking with her. "But you've always been a good sport about it, haven't you?" he said, when he came up for air.

"Yeah, Brandon's a good sport," Nate said. "Hey, Brandon, I'll let you make out with Sherry if you want to."

"Hey!" Sherry swatted Nate across his chest.

"Oh, come on, Sherry. Share a little." That made the Four Horrors laugh. "Sharin' Sherry. Share it around. Share and Sherry alike."

Brandon laughed, too.

"Go on, Brandon. Do what you like to do with Joanne. Call it a peace offering from us. We really did like you all those years."

They really *did* like him.

Nate gave Sherry a little push, and Sherry went along, putting her lips to Brandon's. It set off explosions all through Brandon's brain and body. His arm went around her.

"Not too much, Brandon," Nate said. "Remember, she's just a loaner."

In the next instant, Sherry was back with Nate, but they were all laughing. And they were including Brandon in the game.

"Maybe you should transfer to our school," Dwayne said. He took a little plastic bag and some papers out of his pocket, and rolled a joint. He put a match to it, breathed in, and said, "We're getting up a boxing team, but the school can't afford a punching bag." He let the smoke out in a snort, laughing at his own joke.

Brandon laughed with the rest of them.

"I'm hungry," Sherry said. "I need chocolate, or popcorn, or that popcorn with caramel on it. What's that called?"

"Fiddle Faddle," Sylvie said, taking a drag on the joint. "Fiddle Faddle," she said again, which made everyone laugh and laugh.

"You got any money on you, Brandon?"

Brandon pulled all the coins out of his pocket. There was a bunch of bigger coins mixed in with the smaller ones, the ones that weren't worth as much. Money took concentration. Dimes were worth more than nickels, but they were smaller. It didn't make any sense. He handed it all over to Dwayne.

"Thanks, Brandon. Now all we need is a store."

"Fiddle Faddle!" Sylvie yelled. "Fiddle Faddle!" It turned into a chant.

They all started shouting, "Fiddle Faddle! Fiddle Faddle!"

Just as Brandon opened his mouth to join in, Dwayne put his arm back and threw all of the coins up onto the roof of the school. Brandon heard them fall.

"Think you can get onto the roof?" Dwayne asked him.

"You get those coins off the roof, and I'll let you make out with Sherry again," Nate said.

Sherry gave Nate another swat and said, "He kisses better than you do. Keep loaning me out and I may stay that way. Owww!" she screeched, as Nate twisted her fingers back.

"Up you go, Brandon. We're still hungry."

Brandon started looking for a drainpipe or some other way to boost himself up, but he never got the chance.

The gleam of headlights started to approach from the side driveway.

"*Cops*," said Nate.

"Here, Brandon. Hold this for us and keep your mouth shut. And then you can be our friend." Dwayne tucked the little plastic bag with the marijuana in it into the front pocket of Brandon's jeans, just as the police car rounded the corner of the school.

Friends, thought Brandon, happily. *I have friends.*

His mother hadn't ruined everything, after all.

Lunch with Lenin

Valerin is five.

He waits and waits beside his mother for the bus to
come, and he holds tightly to her hand as they climb
on. There are no spare seats, and the lady who is
sitting beside where he stands doesn't like children, or
doesn't like him. She frowns whenever he puts his
hand on her coat to steady himself against the rocking
of the bus.

They leave the bus and go into the Metro, down,
down, down, deep into the earth on escalators so steep
he is sure they will flip over and hurl them all into the
darkness. He starts to whimper and his mother yanks
on his arm to stop him.

After the Metro they go back on the escalators,
up this time. And then there is a lot of walking, or it
seems like a lot as the day is chilly and gray, and

Valerin doesn't know where they are going or when they will get there.

They stop at a vendor's cart, and his mother buys him some ice cream on a stick, with chocolate all around it. "I want you to have a good day," she says, then she fusses about the drips he is getting on his jacket.

They sit on benches in front of the Tomb of the Unknown Soldier and watch the honor guard make their slow march from one side of the eternal flame to the other. The high wall of the Kremlin is right behind them. It looks like a prison wall, and Valerin wonders for a moment if his father is behind that wall or some other wall. But he doesn't think about that for long. He has his ice cream, and by sitting on the bench he can swing his feet, which makes them not hurt so much. His heavy, brown shoes are scuffed and tight, and he wonders if today will be the day when he finally gets new ones.

They start walking again, and Valerin shows his mother how grown-up he is by putting his ice-cream stick in the trash basket. There are a lot of people around now, and Valerin and his mother go with the crowd under an archway and into a big, empty space.

His mother bends down to speak to him. "This is Red Square," she tells him. "People come to Russia from all over the world to see it."

Valerin is not impressed. It isn't red and it isn't

square—he knows about shapes—but it is BIG. He feels lost and small inside it, even though there are a lot of people walking around. He pulls on his mother's arm.

"Can we go home now?"

Instead, they walk deeper into Red Square.

There is a big, black, windowless building on one side of the square.

"You sit here," his mother says, and she buys him another ice cream. "I'll just go in and pay my respects to Comrade Lenin." She bends down to button the top of his jacket again and to tell him to be a good boy while she is in there. "It's not something you'll understand yet. You'll see him when you're older. Stay right here and wait for Mommy."

He stays where she puts him and waits like she says, only he undoes that top button because it's too tight and chokes him.

He starts to eat the ice cream, but he doesn't really want it because he just had one. He doesn't know what to do with it because his mother took the paper wrapper away with her. He can't look for a trash can because he'd have to walk away from the spot where she told him to wait. The chocolate coating begins to slip down the stick as the ice cream melts, and he starts to feel sticky. He's worried that his clothes will get messed up. He tries to eat it quickly, but he really doesn't want it and it makes him feel sick. He puts what's left down on the bricks and tries to hide it with his shoes. He waits and waits.

The day gets darker and colder. He has to go to the toilet really bad, and then he doesn't anymore, but now he's wet and colder, and his mother will really be mad. The square that's not a square is empty, and he's still sitting there.

By the time anyone comes to ask about him, he's been waiting nearly two days, and he can't remember the name of the man his mother went to visit. The police try to put him in their police car, and he fights and screams because he doesn't want to be taken to prison and put behind high walls, and because his mother told him to stay there, and she'll be angry that he's moved. But the police are bigger, and they're angry that they have to touch his clothes where he wet himself. They get him into the back of the car and close the door.

Valerin keeps his eyes open wide as they drive away from Red Square, certain that his mother will come running up, demanding to know why he didn't do as he was told.

Valerin is seven.

He sits on the floor of the hallway in a row with the other boys and waits his turn. He sits very still in case his mother shows up. There are noises from the other children, but no words. Valerin knows words, he even uses them sometimes, but he hasn't spoken for a long time and gradually has forgotten the point of it.

He has made a room in his head where he lives. His mother is there, bringing him soup and *blinis*, and she reads to him from a book about a bear, moving her finger along the words as she says them so he can learn his letters. He remembers this over and over, until he can smell soup instead of old urine. And he can hear her voice instead of the squeals of the children around him. He feels the softness of his pajamas instead of the hands of the caretaker, which are not rough or mean, just used to bathing kids quickly. He is stripped and bathed and toweled down with the efficiency of a fish-gutter in a processing plant. He doesn't notice.

He spends the morning in the dayroom on a chair. Around him, the other children are rocking because there is nothing else to do. Valerin feels the movement of the rocking around him and joins in. Back and forth, like the pendulum on a grandfather clock.

One day, outsiders arrive, cheerful and loud. They bring bananas and songs and ask the matron questions that make her frown. One of them, a lady, gets right down in front of Valerin so his eyes must meet hers. She is almost too pretty.

"These are for you."

She hands him crayons—a whole box—and a scribbler with a picture of a smiling cow on the cover.

Valerin is slow to make a connection. The wires in his brain are rusty.

The woman opens the box and puts a crayon in his hand, a red crayon, and opens the scribbler to the first page.

"For you," she says. "To draw nice pictures."

The wires spark. Valerin remembers how to hold a crayon. He puts marks into the scribbler, and the marks come together to form something his mother made him practice over and over until he could do it perfectly.

He writes his name.

Valerin is nine.

A breezy, efficient woman with a zippered file folder under her arm has him firmly by the hand, even though he tries to pull away, to get back into the car. Already he can hear jeers from the kids looking down at him from the orphanage window.

"I want to go back," he says, trying to dig his heels into the cement walk.

"They don't want you back," the woman says. "You don't belong there. Do you know how much trouble I've gone to, getting you moved?" She presses the doorbell and pulls him inside. She puts him into a chair in the foyer. "Wait here."

He waits.

"Why don't you run?" someone says to him.

He looks up. A boy, lean and fluid like water on legs, is leaning against the banister. "Door's not locked from the inside. Why don't you run?"

Valerin looks at the boy's face, but can't tell if the smile is kind or mean—it's sort of sad and sort of friendly, but Valerin isn't good at reading smiles. Instead, he turns to look at the door. He can't imagine just walking through it by himself. He can't remember ever doing such a thing.

The breezy woman is back, and he's taken into an office and talked to and frowned at. And then the breezy woman is gone without a good-bye. Valerin didn't know her, and he doesn't miss her.

He is taken to a dormitory with twelve beds. He curls up on the first one and starts to cry. He's thrown off the bed by a pack of kids. They watch him make his way down the row of beds, throwing him off each one until he comes to the last one in the row. They leave him alone then and run down to their suppers.

"You're from the idiots' home," someone says. "You must be pretty special. They don't usually admit when they've made a mistake."

Valerin waits for the insult, but when it doesn't come, he rolls over to see who is talking to him. It is the boy from the hall.

"I'm not special," Valerin says.

"I listen in at doors," the boy says. "No other way to learn anything around here." He sits down on the bed beside Valerin's. "You don't talk for two years, and all of a sudden you write your name without being taught. They think you might be some kind of genius."

"I'm not," Valerin says. He doesn't want any trouble.

"We'll see," says the other boy. He gets to his feet. "Come on, before it's all gone."

"What?"

"Supper, of course."

Valerin says, "I'm not hungry." But he is.

"They won't bother you if you're with me. They're afraid of me. I'm unpredictable." He gets to the dormitory door and turns around. "I'm waiting."

Valerin gets off his bed and joins the boy at the door.

"My name's Squid," says the boy. "They don't like me, either."

Valerin is twelve.

He's learned a little bit at school.

He's learned a lot at the orphanage.

He's learned that the kids who still have a parent who keeps in touch by visiting or sending letters and parcels are worth more than the kids who don't. And the kids whose parents are both dead are worth more than the ones whose parents don't want them anymore. Valerin gets no letters, parcels, or visits. He is at the bottom of the heap. Damaged goods.

He is easy prey for the higher-up kids. On video night they watch Leonardo DiCaprio slip into the ocean, and they ask Valerin about his mother.

"She went down with the *Titanic*," he says. Other times, he says, "She's a cosmonaut," or, "She's with the Security Police."

There is no teasing about fathers, though. None of the children have fathers. Fathers disappear. It's what they all do, no insult to the children. But a mother disappearing!

"There must be something really wrong with you," the others tell Valerin over and over.

He wonders if he should have left his top button done up. He wonders if he should have eaten all his ice cream and put the stick into a trash basket. He can't think of anything else he's done wrong.

The other kids bully him. They push him down and hide or steal his belongings. He gets in trouble with the matron for wearing the same shirt over and over, and she has no patience when he tells her the other shirts have disappeared.

Every afternoon the children who go to the local school stream back into the orphanage, full of the insults they've taken from the children whose parents still want them, eager to pass those hurts on to someone else. Valerin is the one they usually choose.

Unless Squid is around. No one bothers Valerin then.

Valerin can't understand it at first. Squid has never fought anyone outright, never threatened anyone, never ratted anyone out.

Then, one day, a gang of girls who have been tormenting Valerin all day go back to their dorm to find that their teddy bears have all been decapitated. The heads of the bears turn up a week later, stuck on the spikes of the fence that closes in the orphanage.

Valerin walks a little taller. He stays close to Squid. He gets by.

Valerin is thirteen.

"You think she'll still be waiting for you, don't you?" Squid asks.

They are cleaning out the bathrooms as punishment for being difficult. The others are on an outing to the Moscow Circus. The janitor has turned over his mops and brushes to them before retreating to his basement room with a bottle. They have the place to themselves. And Squid asks the question again.

"You think she'll still be waiting for you, don't you?"

"No, I don't," says Valerin.

"You think either she'll come here to get you or she's hanging around Red Square, waiting for you to show up."

"I don't think about it."

"You don't talk about it, either. I have to learn about your life by breaking into the office to read your file. I've told you about my life—mother dead, father drunk, end of story. But you don't tell me about yours because you think she still loves you."

"No," says Valerin, seeing that Squid is between him and the door.

"Then tell me."

Valerin tries to fade away into the old grayness, but Squid is having none of that. He pushes Valerin into a corner and slides him down the tile wall to the floor. He holds Valerin's face between his hands.

"Tell me."

Valerin tells. The first time, it comes out with tears and wails, like vomit.

"Tell me again," says Squid.

The second time hurts just as bad. By the fifth time, it hurts slightly less.

They keep at it. By the end of the day, Valerin doesn't feel anything. He recites the story as if it were a history lesson about strangers long, long ago and far, far away.

The others will be back soon. Squid knows where one of the girls has hidden the box of chocolates she got from her mother. They eat them all, then put the empty box beside the drunk and sleeping janitor.

Six months later, Squid turns sixteen.

The day after that, he is gone.

Valerin is fifteen.

"You'll be sixteen in one week, as near as we can tell," the head of the orphanage says from behind his desk. "You came to us without papers, so we have to guess. At any rate, we're moving you. You'll get the government stipend due to orphans, a room in Shcherbinka, and an apprenticeship to an auto mechanic. Try to learn something useful. It will smooth your way when you enter the army." He hands Valerin some papers. "I can't say it's been good having you here, but I wish you luck with the rest of your life."

He picks up his pen and Valerin is dismissed.

Valerin turns sixteen without ceremony and packs what little he has into the sports bag he's been given.

The matron holds out a postcard.

It's his first mail. He holds it and stares, hardly believing. On the front is a cartoon of a Russian bear in a bikini, with the words "Moscow Bathing Beauty" printed along the bottom. He turns it over.

The message is short: *Meet me in Red Square at noon*, along with a date two Saturdays from now. It's signed, *Squid*.

"Take care of yourself," the matron says. "When you get out there, you'll realize we weren't so bad."

❧

Valerin has a room to himself—tiny, but it's his own—in a boarding house in an ugly neighborhood. The bathroom is shared by all the tenants. The landlady refuses to cook for him and refuses to show him how, so he goes without until he can gather enough information by watching the others.

"You orphanage boys, you're all useless," the land-lady says, sitting down at the kitchen table to give her World War Two medals their weekly polish. She was a sniper in the battle of Stalingrad, something she reminds him of daily. "You don't know how to make tea, you don't know how to do laundry. You are used to having everything done for you. Well, now you're in the real world!"

During the day, Valerin works in the mechanics garage, sweeping and staying out of the way. At night he stays on his bed and waits for time to pass.

The Saturday arrives when Valerin is to meet up with Squid. He takes the train to Moscow, then the underground to Okhotny Ryad Station. He stands outside Resurrection Gate before entering Red Square. He leans against a wall and lets a herd of tourists brush past him into the square. There is no need to rush in with them. He is early, and a little afraid.

"Help me! Help me!"

Valerin looks down. At his feet is a woman with a swaddled child lying listlessly across her lap. Another child, a boy no older than five, holds out his little hand in a mirrored action of his mother's, begging for rubles.

Valerin feels suddenly sick. He stumbles away from the child and his mother, knocking into the English-speaking tourists with their cameras and guidebooks and noisy complaints.

He forces himself to stand still. The bricks are laid out in a pattern under his feet. He is standing where armies have marched. The monarchists, anarchists, communists, and capitalists have all pounded these bricks in celebration, defiance, or mourning.

He recalls more from the photos he's seen than from his own memory. On his right, stands the historical museum. On his left, the long, white, majestic GUM Department Store.

And then, Valerin looks past the spirals of St. Basil's Cathedral to the ugly, black, windowless building along the high wall of the Kremlin. Lenin's Tomb. He moves toward it, past the bench where he sat, all those years ago. Not an ice-cream wrapper in sight.

There is a short lineup of people waiting to enter the tomb. Valerin joins it.

"Where's your ticket? You have to buy a ticket," the guard says, pointing to a kiosk.

Valerin doesn't like spending the money. The stipend from the government isn't very much. But he pays anyway.

It is dark inside. He follows the others down the stairs, into the belly of the tomb, not stopping, the guards moving them along. The line snakes out into a great room, still dark, the only light shining in and over a glass sarcophagus. Inside, laid out like he is asleep, is the man Valerin's mother had gone to see. Comrade Vladimir Ilyich Lenin, the Father of the Revolution. And no one else.

Valerin wants to get out of there. He doesn't want to walk all around the glass case to see the dead leader from all sides. He wants to push through the crowd. He wants to throw something hard, to smash the glass.

Instead, he moves with the line, listening to people whispering, wondering if it's really Lenin or just a wax dummy. It is a relief to get back outside.

"This way to Stalin's grave," the guard says at the exit. "The graves of John Reed and Nikita Khrushchev, right this way, included in your ticket."

Guide chains keep the tourists filing past the other dead leaders, but Valerin has had enough. He checks to see that the guard isn't looking, then hops over the chains.

He sits down on his old bench and puts his face in his hands. He tries to stop himself from shaking.

"Don't you want to see Stalin?" a man asks. "Don't you want to lay flowers on his grave and bless his memory?"

Valerin turns toward the voice and thinks he's gone mad. Sitting on a low wall close by, smoking a cigarette, is Comrade Lenin.

"Taking a break," Lenin says. "Bloody western tourists keep gloating over the end of the Cold War. You smoke yet?"

Valerin shakes his head.

"Well, come join me over here anyway. You look

like someone's just punched the guts out of you. You know, there are only ghosts in there. Even an idiot orphan boy should know that."

Valerin's heart starts to thump, then he looks closer at Lenin's smirking face. "Squid?"

"Comrade Squid. Show some respect." He slaps Valerin on the back. "I've been waiting for you, my friend, and now here you are! Have some lunch." Squid opens up the paper sack that sits on the wall beside him. "I brought extra, hoping you'd show."

There is bread, cheese, and salami sausage. They chew on their lunch and watch the activity in the square. The sunny day has brought people out. Lenin/Squid waves to Trotsky, posing with tourists in front of St. Basil's. "Karl Marx is somewhere around here, too," Squid says. "He doesn't do so well with the tourists. They don't know who he is. And he looks too much like any old drunk."

It doesn't really matter what comes next, Valerin thinks. *I'm happy.*

"Finish the lunch," Squid says. "Eat every bite. I know you orphan boys are always hungry. Watch me work for a while. Then we'll go somewhere."

Valerin stays on the wall, finishing the sausage and watching Lenin, Trotsky, and even poor old Karl Marx handle the tourists and take their money.

The afternoon passes quickly in the warm sun. When the square starts to empty out, Squid collects Valerin and they head back out through Resurrection Gate.

"We have to make a quick stop on the Arbat so I can change my clothes," Squid says. "You don't mind, do you?"

Valerin is happy to go with him anywhere. They walk down Ulitsa Vozdvizhenka, past the Russian State Library, through the pedestrian underpass full of merchants and beggars, and out on a street without cars.

"All the tourists come here to shop," Squid says. "The street used to belong to real artists and thinkers. People like that can't afford Moscow anymore."

He guides Valerin down a walkway between a table full of nesting dolls painted like old Soviet leaders and an American 1950s-style diner, and up a narrow flight of steps. Two other Lenins are already there, in various stages of Lenin-ness.

"Meet my friend, Valerin," Squid says. "Valerin, meet the Architects of the Revolution."

Valerin watches as Squid strips away the communist costume. He gasps at his friend's naked face. It was always thin, but now it's gaunt, skin over skeleton. Squid looks like an old man.

"Maybe I should have let *you* finish the sausage," he says.

Squid laughs, playfully slapping Valerin's face. He grabs his jacket. "Let's go."

Squid manages the Metro with confidence, changing trains, knowing where to go. Valerin sticks close by, paying attention. Someday he will be like this.

They get off the Metro at Park Kultury and cross a bridge over a river.

"We're going to Gorky Park, my friend," Squid says. "Best ride in the world in Gorky Park."

The two young men stride through the gates of Gorky Park like young czars. Inside are trees and flowers and fountains and musical rides and delicious smells.

Valerin is prepared to part with his whole month's stipend right there. He wants to go with his friend on a dozen rides and share a dozen treats. But Squid keeps them walking, past roller coasters and waterslides, past things that go around and things that go up and down.

"There it is," Squid says, pointing ahead to a giant, slow-moving Ferris wheel. "The Gates of Heaven."

Valerin digs into his pocket for rubles, but Squid puts his hand on Valerin's arm to stop him.

"First one's on me," he says. "A liberation present." He motions for Valerin to hang back and goes up and talks to the guy in the ticket booth. He comes back smiling.

"Do we line up?" Valerin asks.

Instead of answering, Squid leads him up a little hill into a thicket of trees. A shed sits among the pines. Squid knocks and the door is opened.

There isn't much light coming through the one little window, but among the snow shovels and sacks of ice melter, Valerin counts five people. They are stretched out on the sacks. Someone inhales smoke from a water pipe and passes it on. Others are just lying there.

"Got works?" Squid asks.

A man with a bad cough and sores on his skin is injecting something into his arm with a hypodermic needle. He sighs back against the wall with the needle still stuck in his skin. Squid gently takes the needle out and loosens the rubber band from around the man's arm.

"The Gates of Heaven, the Gates of Heroin," Squid says, jiggling two little white packets in front of Valerin's face. "This is my gift to you. It takes away the sins of the world, as least for a little while. And folks wonder what Russia ever got out of the war with Afghanistan."

Squid prepares the solution and fills the syringe. "Roll up your sleeve," he says to Valerin.

"No," says Valerin. Maybe he would if he were alone with Squid. Maybe he would if they'd had their day of fun, and this was at the end of it. But he doesn't like this shed, and he doesn't like these people.

"Let's go," he urges. "Let's go get some dinner. I've got my stipend. We'll get a good meal and celebrate."

Squid doesn't answer except to roll up his own sleeve and plunge the needle in. He leans his head back as the drug floods his body. Valerin sees the shadows and hollows of Squid's thin face.

"You're not well, Squid," Valerin says. "Come home with me. I'll take care of you."

But Squid doesn't answer. He's far, far away.

Valerin turns away and leaves the shed. He steps out into the late afternoon sun. As he looks around, Valerin wonders what to do next. He has money in his pocket. He could enjoy the park. He could get back on the Metro and go home to Shcherbinka.

He could go out to the middle of the bridge and throw himself in the river.

Instead, he does the one thing he is best at. The one thing it seems he is meant to do. He sits down against a tree, where he can keep an eye on the shed door.

And he waits.

Boot

The van door opens and I fall off the face of the Earth.

"Out! Move! Now!"

The eight of us, three girls and five guys, stumble out. Our legs are shackled and our hands are cuffed in front of us. We fall, we get up, we try to run where they tell us. But there are so many of them yelling, and they're yelling different orders. It takes a while before we're all lined up on the red dots painted on the concrete yard. I stare at the high fence with its rows of barbed wire at the top.

The warden stands in front of us. He is a tall, stocky man, and he's wearing some sort of green uniform—an army wannabe, I guess.

"You have all agreed to come here in exchange for a shorter sentence," he says, instead of a hello. "One-third of you will quit before your stay here is up, and you will be shipped back to your originating prison to complete your full sentence. If we decide you are not cooperating, back to the regular prison you will go. Time spent here will not count."

He walks up and down the line, staring hard at each of us. I have a headache. My last hit is wearing off. Kicker smuggled it into the county jail on his last visit, and it wasn't much. My head really hurts. Coffee will help. I wonder when we'll get some.

"In my prison, there are no video nights, no pizza parties, and no one cares about your feelings," the warden says. "Your rehabilitation is up to you. The taxpayers are fed up with you, so we're not wasting anything new on you. Your barracks are old army Quonset huts. Your uniforms and bunks are old army discards. Your sheets and towels were tossed in the trash by the State Hospital.

"They call this place the Boot, and let me tell you why. If you cross me, I will land like a boot on your neck. And I will stay there until you are broken." Even through the hangover, I figure he's laying it on a bit thick.

And then the others are yelling and screaming again as our shackles and handcuffs are taken off and we are made to run into a Quonset hut and stand in two lines, boys on one side, girls on the other. That's what they call us, although the boys are old enough to shave, and I know for sure that at least one of the girls is somebody's mother.

I end up first in the girls' line.

"Sit." I am ordered into a chair in the middle of the room. I sit. I don't see the clippers until they are running through my hair, plowing it down to the bare skull. The shock makes me start to rise to my feet.

"Move and I'll cut off your ear."

I stay put. There are no mirrors in the room, but I close my eyes anyway. I hear the clippers whine and feel my hair fall away. My long, curly red hair—the object of envy and lust, recipient of expensive products—is all gone now. Garbage on the floor, waiting to be swept up.

"Run," someone orders, and I run, in the wrong direction. Someone else yells at me until I figure out that I'm supposed to run to an alcove and strip. My clothes are bagged and tagged, "In case you ever get out of here." I'm prepared for this—it happened at the county jail, too—and I get through the cavity check by pretending I'm somewhere else.

The water landing on my bare head in the shower is startling, foreign. I keep my hands off my head. I don't want to touch my smooth scalp. I can't believe it's legal to cut off someone's hair, and I wonder who I can complain to.

A pile of dingy fatigues is dumped in my arms. I dress and sit on a bench. First one, then the other girl joins me. They look like aliens, with heads like bowling balls and eyes red from crying. I'm glad I didn't cry. There's no way I look like them.

I'm assigned to a platoon of fifty girls. "These are the inmates you will march with, work with, eat with, and share a dormitory with." The platoon captain is a character straight out of Central Casting. She starts talking about the schedule and the rules.

The pain in my head is worse. I raise my hand. "I have a headache," I say. "Could I get some Tylenol or aspirin or something?"

What I get is the guard's face up close to mine, eyeball to eyeball.

"You are all here because you act without thinking!" she shouts. "And if you do think, you only think about yourselves. For the duration of your stay here, you will not use the word *I*. If you *must* refer to yourself, you will say, 'This prisoner.' Do I make myself CLEAR?"

What's clear is that I'm not getting any painkillers or a cup of coffee or anything other than the guard's spit in my face and sore muscles from running from one place to another.

We spend the first afternoon learning how to march, stepping on each other's heels and being screamed at for our mistakes.

It's Friday, I realize suddenly. It's party night. My friends are getting ready. They've skipped afternoon classes and are laying down a base of alcohol. They're lying to parents and scoring drugs—not difficult, thanks to Kicker.

"I'll send you something to make it easier," he promised me on that last visit. "We'll all write," my friends said. "We'll send you chocolates with surprise centers and magazines and cigarettes." They made it sound like I was going away to summer camp.

"Eyes front! Who told you to daydream?"

Why do the guards have to stand so close? I take a step back. She steps right along with me. "Drop and give me twenty!"

Twenty what? Is she kidding?

"Twenty push-ups, prisoner. Do them! Now!"

The pavement is rough, with little pebbles that hurt the palms of my hands. My head *pounds* with the movement of my body. All the time, the guard keeps screaming. "Is this the way you're going to start out? Is this the way you're going to continue? You think you can come into my platoon and pull this crap? You *will* give me twenty push-ups!"

By the time the guard lets me up, I am a scared, sobbing mess with snot running down my face. I'm glad no one I know is here to witness this.

They march us into dinner—some kind of vile stew on a hunk of corn bread. Guards yell at kids who try to throw food away. I drown the mess in ketchup and choke it down. We eat in silence. I keep my eyes on my plate and off the bald heads around me. I try not to think about my friends.

After supper we are marched some more. Then we run to the barracks for Confrontation.

"You are expected to rat on each other," the platoon captain says. She stands at the front of the room while all fifty of us sit stiffly on benches. No slouching is allowed.

"If you see someone doing something they shouldn't, and you don't report it, you will be punished. If you are the first to tell us of a transgression, you may get a reward. A cookie with lunch. A fifteen-minute rest break in the middle of a work detail. Things you will come to appreciate as luxuries here at the Boot."

Immediately, a girl jumps to her feet.

"This Prisoner Chapelle wishes to state that she saw Prisoner Williams slacking off during Physical Training."

"Prisoner Williams. Front and center."

Prisoner Williams, whose first name I don't know, marches to the front of the room and spins sharply on her heels.

"Is this true?"

"Yes, Captain."

"Drop and do twenty-five."

I watch in fascination as girl after girl stands up to accuse other platoon members. On and on it goes. I can't believe the enthusiasm. Lots of girls snitch on each other. Now and then a guard hands out a coupon for a cookie, an extra water break, or ten minutes with a newspaper.

The rewards suck. Why do they bother? It's like kindergarten—everyone eager to tattle to the teacher.

At 8:15, we run to the lavatory for a final wash, then into the dormitory. The large room is divided by cubicles that reach as high as my neck. I look out over a sea of disembodied bald heads sticking up over the walls. Each cubicle has a bunk bed and two small cupboards. I am assigned a top bunk. To sleep, we wear t-shirts and army skivvies. Everything is done in silence, and by whistle. I keep my eyes on my bunk mate to learn what to do. One whistle blast and we stand at attention by our beds. Two blasts and we change quickly, folding our clothes and putting them away on a shelf in a small cupboard. Then we stand at attention again. Three blasts and we hop into bed, sitting bolt upright, legs under the covers.

A guard recites a prayer. "We thank you, oh Lord, for the opportunity to become good citizens and to stop disappointing the people who love us. Amen."

Then, in unison, all the girls put their heads on their pillows, the lights go out, and there is silence.

It is 8:30.

The party at home is just getting started. I stare up into the semidarkness. I try to take my mind there— to the music, the dancing, the money I would make selling drugs for Kicker. I almost manage it. I've almost transported myself when the guard barks at a girl for asking to go to the latrine without using the proper wording: "This Prisoner Jackson requests permission..." The party disappears, and I am back in prison.

I fight off, of all things, homesickness. They didn't come to see me after I was sentenced, so why should I think of them now? They won't rescue me. None of these other girls have been rescued by their families. The forty-nine restless bodies in the bunks around me sigh, cry out in their sleep, or sniff into their pillows. And all night long, a guard sits at an elevated table, watching our torment.

It's a long night, but the darkness and the quiet

soothe my head, and I manage to drift away from time to time. I realize that here, sleep will be my best friend.

The morning siren goes off. Glaring florescent lights go on above us. Guards bang their truncheons on our metal bunks. All around me, the girls sit up and yell like new recruits in a bad army movie. We leap to attention at the entrance to our cubicles for the morning count.

Then it's a mad dash to the latrines, where there are no mirrors, thank God. And we jump into our sweats and run into line. I get mixed up. I forget who I'm supposed to stand behind—all the bald heads look alike—and I get my first reprimand of the day. The clock reads 4:35.

We jog out of our barracks into the chilled morning air and join the other platoons on the parade grounds for PT and a run. I don't want the guys to see me with my head shaved, even though I don't know them, even though everyone else's head is shaved, including all of theirs.

Spotlights shine down on us from above—a whole yard full of bald-headed kids doing push-ups, sit-ups, jumping jacks, and lunges.

"For those of you who have just arrived, I'll explain," the warden says through a megaphone. "You are standing in front of the Supermax Unit of the prison. Some of you will end up in this building because you are unwilling to change your lives. In this building, you will be confined to your cell twenty-three hours a day. I guarantee that when you are sitting there, listening to me make this little speech every morning, you will wish you had taken advantage of the opportunity you have here today."

Then he starts reciting something and everyone joins in. It's some kind of motto.

Every morning in Africa, a gazelle wakes up.

It knows it must run faster than the fastest lion, or it will be killed.

Every morning, a lion wakes up also.

It knows it must outrun the slowest gazelle or it will starve to death.

It doesn't matter whether you are a lion or a gazelle.

When the sun comes up, you had better be running.

Then, we run.

I was on the track-and-field team in junior high, but by high school I had Kicker and other things to think about. The run is slow, but I still lag behind, and no amount of screaming by the guards will make me move faster. My headache is gone, but my mood isn't good, and I step it up just to avoid punching someone.

Lunch is more swill on a shingle. Then it is time for Stripes.

"These are the Stripes of Shame," the platoon captain says, holding up a smock with bold black and white stripes across it and a big letter *P* on the back. "These are the only garments made especially for this prison. Some of you will make them during your work duty. You wear these while performing community service. They show the taxpayers of this state that their money is being well spent. Today, this platoon will be picking up trash in a city park. You will be chained. You will be guarded. And you will be silent. Any attempt to engage in conversation with a non-prisoner will be interpreted as an attempt to escape. And you do not want that."

I put on my smock. We are loaded into trucks, and I'm shackled to the girl next to me.

"This place is *G.I. Jane* meets *Cool Hand Luke*," the girl says quietly, when the guard is busy chaining someone else. I notice that her hair is fuzzy with stubble and I wonder how long it will take for mine to grow that much. "I used to work in a video store," she says. "I saw everything."

"I saw *Cool Hand Luke* on the movie channel once," I whisper back.

"Everything old is new again. I'm Julie Martin. I sleep under you but you probably didn't notice. Cocaine possession. I was holding it for my stupid boyfriend."

"Krysta Walters," I introduce myself. "Busted selling ecstasy to an undercover. For my boyfriend."

"Two smart operators," says Julie. "Most girls are in here because of their crappy taste in guys."

The guard comes closer and we shut up.

I'm glad the Boot is on the other side of the state from my home. No one I know is likely to see me here, chained to a row of girls, all dressed alike, all bald heads and prison caps. The guards hand us garbage bags, and we go to work, cleaning up one area, and then moving as a group to another. The park is one of those neighborhood parks, with moms and kids at swings and old people on benches. And some teens cutting class and smoking on top of picnic tables, just like I used to, back when I was free.

"That's what will happen to you if you keep being bad." A mother is talking to her two small daughters. The girls stare at me, fingers in their mouths. With their mother right behind them, they have more curiosity than fear.

"You were bad," the biggest of the little girls says, pointing at me and giggling. She picks up a handful of grass and throws it at me. Her younger sister does the same, and tufts of dead leaves, sticks, and pebbles fly in my direction. Their mother doesn't stop them.

At the halfway point in the afternoon, one by one we are unchained and taken to the park's bathroom.

When I wash my hands, I get my first look at my new self in the mirror. My ears and eyes are too big and my head is too small. I don't recognize myself. There's nothing of me that stares back in the reflection. None of it seems real.

Two girls my age—not prisoners, real girls—come in and start to fuss with their hair and makeup. They catch me staring at them, and they also see the guard behind me, gripping my clothes so I can't run away. They go silent, and when I am yanked back out to the chain gang, I can hear the laughter burst out of them. It sounds like the laughter that's burst out of me when I've made fun of someone I didn't care about hurting.

I don't know those girls, I say to myself. *None of this will get back to my friends.* It's small comfort.

This evening is the same as the last, and the next day is the same as this one. I stop being a newbie when some of the girls graduate—or get kicked out—and replacements are brought in to fill their bunks. On Sundays, there's mandatory chapel. On days we don't do Stripes, we do schoolwork. And then there's Addictions Work; this consists mostly of plowing through thick workbooks, where we read about the affects of marijuana and other illegal drugs on our brains and fill in units like "List the names of the people you have hurt."

We don't think anybody actually reads the notebooks. We figure they just check to make sure that we've filled in the blanks with *something*. One of the girls adds "Mickey Mouse" and "Donald Trump" to her list, and she gets into so much trouble that the rest of us do our work as we are supposed to.

I can do six months of this, I tell myself, over and over.

It's six months of this or three years in prison.

I can do six months of this.

The faces of my platoon-mates become recognizable. I even begin to forget that we should have hair. We get shaved once a month, so just when I start to feel normal again, it's gone. There's no hope of looking good when I get out. Maybe I can pretend I've had cancer and my hair fell out with the chemo.

The only letters that come are from my family, and I throw those away without reading them. The letters come to me already open, and I begin to suspect that the guards are keeping the gifts my friends promised to send.

"No gifts allowed," Julie says, when I grumble to her. "No candy, no magazines, no letters except from family. Didn't they tell you?"

"They can't tamper with the mail," I say. "That's a crime."

Julie just smiles and goes back to folding her laundry according to regulations, stacking it neatly in her little cupboard. She's been here for three months and has given up.

"And this Confrontation thing," I whisper. I'm on a roll and keep talking, even though I risk getting Julie into trouble. "Why is everyone so enthusiastic?"

Julie does a quick check on the guard. He's yelling at someone on the other side of the dormitory. "When else do we get to talk?" she asks.

It's true. No talking is the rule for all day, every day, unless we're asked a direct question by one of the guards. We find ways—a comment or two here and there. But whispered and furtive, not a real conversation. I know almost nothing about the girls in my platoon, except that they all seem to have given up. Now and then someone will stand up to a guard or refuse to get out of bed or try to flirt with someone from the boys' platoons (*absolutely* forbidden), but mostly they all go along to get along.

"We're just doing their work for them," I say. "In Confrontation, I mean. Wouldn't it be great if we all stop, if no one has anything to say?"

"They've been at this a lot longer than you have," Julie says, then she walks away from me to report to the guard that her laundry is put away.

I get an idea. Every prison needs a hero, someone who will stand up to the system. It's in all the prison movies. They can send me back to regular prison for *doing* something, but how could they punish me for *not* doing something, not talking in Confrontation?

I'd get everyone else to keep silent—even just once! That will show these guards who's really in charge. The captain will ask, "Who has something to bring to our attention?" and we will all sit in absolute silence, staring straight ahead while the captain bellows and screams.

I laugh out loud at the thought of it—not too loud. And for the next two days, every time I think of it, I get a hot rush of excitement. I think about it so intensely that I complete the five-mile run without having to stop once to catch my breath.

I start to mention it to a few girls during Stripes, when we're pulling trash from the yard and gardens around a hospital. It's easiest to talk then.

"Let's all be silent during Confrontation," I say. "Why should we turn on each other? It's us against them, not us against us." They all say it's a good idea and they'll pass it along.

Confrontation comes, and I'm sitting on the hard bench, back straight, waiting for the fun to begin.

"Who has something to report?" the platoon captain asks.

Prisoner Faber raises her hand, and marches out,

front and center. "This Prisoner Faber wishes to state that Prisoner Walters was urging her to remain silent during Confrontation."

Another hand goes up, and another. One by one, all the girls I spoke to—except Julie—proudly rat me out in exchange for a coupon for one lousy store-bought oatmeal cookie.

"Do you think you are smarter than we are, Prisoner?" the captain yells at me as I stand alone in front of the whole platoon. "Is this the same brilliant thinking that landed you in here? Do you really think you can disrupt the smooth running of my platoon? It's sandwich boards for you. Two weeks."

I find out what sandwich boards are at the next meal. I have to stand in the dining hall with two heavy boards hanging from my shoulders. The boards read, "Anti-Social." I have to eat while I stand. It's uncomfortable and embarrassing. I know everyone is looking at me, and for the first few days, I keep my eyes down so I don't have to see them staring. When I finally start looking around, I realize that I am being totally ignored. Everyone else's eyes are down. I don't know if this makes me feel better or worse. It all feels pretty pointless.

A week into my punishment, I'm joined at the front of the dining hall by a boy. His sandwich boards read,

"Slob." He stands beside me for three days. I never learn his name.

It's a relief when I can finally sit down again to eat. I want to say something about it to my tablemates. I want to ask them if they missed me. But they keep their eyes on their plates.

I flash on all those times my parents wanted me to eat at the table with them, but I'd take my plate to the TV room and turn on some rerun. I don't like to think this way. I make my mind blank and let the routine carry me along.

I even join in the ratting during Confrontation. Nothing major, nothing that gets anyone into real trouble. But after a while I get tired of being screamed at and punished for my lack of participation. I have to start playing along.

"Accuse me," Julie suggests. "Get them off your back."

So I accuse Julie of not lining up her boots properly at night. Julie gets fifteen push-ups, and the guards leave me alone for a while.

After that, the days are all the same. I learn to tune out the screaming guards. My body gets used to the exercise, to the morning siren, to the nasty food, to sleeping soundly in a room with so many others. Life at the Boot starts to feel normal.

I forget my friends' faces. "We'll write to you," they said, but they probably didn't even try. And Kicker has surely found someone else to sell his little pills for him. They're all having fun without me, and I can't remember why I thought they wouldn't.

I stop counting the days, and I don't think too much. The letters from home stop coming. I guess they got tired of writing and never getting a response.

We're deep into summer now, deep into what would have been summer vacation. My platoon is doing Stripes work, chain-ganging along the side of a country road. We've been here for two weeks. People honk at us on their way to the cottage or the lake. Some people do more. Some swear at us and throw things. Prisoner Edson is badly bruised by a full can of Dr. Pepper. Prisoner Ransome gets burned in the face by a lit cigarette.

We even get regulars. As long as they don't try to approach us, the guards don't keep them from stopping nearby. One guy sits in his car and stares at us for an hour before driving away again. It's funny at first, then just creepy. Groups of kids sit on the hood and roof of their cars, making rude comments and throwing fresh trash down for us to pick up.

One lady stops every day to offer us water and juice, which the guards always refuse. She calls out to us, things like, "Days will get better" and "Don't give up hope" and "You're all strong women!" Then she sits in her car and cranks up her CD player so we can have music while we work. It's good music, too. A little old, but still good.

Mostly, I keep my back to the road and pull up the weeds and the garbage. I whisper complaints to my chain-mates about people being jerks, too lazy to toss their McDonald's wrappers into a trash can. I'm embarrassed that I used to do the same thing all the time, way back in my former life.

I am picking up garbage under a tree, trying to ignore the ache in my back, when I hear the chirping.

I look around for the source, and at first I can't find it. Then, as I clear away more weeds and junk, I see it. A baby bird has fallen from its nest.

"Julie," I whisper. "Come and look."

Julie is right there, tugging along the next girl on the chain and the next. And then there are twelve of us on that stretch of chain, all gathered around the little bird.

"It looks like us," someone says, and she's right. The bird is bald, with big eyes, and it can't do anything for itself.

"Let's keep it," Prisoner Thomas suggests. "We'll raise it. A barracks pet."

We start to debate the idea but don't get very far.

"What's going on here? Get back to work! Who told you to take a break?" The guard comes down the line, swinging her truncheon around her head. We break up our circle so she can see what we've found.

The baby bird looks up at our circle of faces and chirps. Scared and sweet.

The guard brings her truncheon down to it, nudging it gently. "It doesn't look hurt," she says. "Just stunned. Where's the nest?"

We look around. We hear more chirping but can't see a nest until we see the mother bird—a starling, I think—heading into a hollow part of the tree.

"You can't touch it with your hands," the guard says. "The mother will reject it. Look around for a bit of board or something flat to scoop it up with."

We spread out, as far as our chains will let us. There's plenty of garbage to choose from. Prisoner Williams finds an old Domino's Pizza box. We work together to tear it into a bird-sized scoop. I try to hand it to the guard.

She shakes her head. "You do it," she says.

Slowly, carefully, we get the bird onto the bit of cardboard. It's hard to get up the tree all chained together. Prisoner Donaldson is the smallest. We all boost her up, and she gently tips the baby bird into the hollow, into the nest with the rest of its family.

"It's home," she says. "We got it home."

We stand around the tree, looking up at the hollow.

"I saw a bluebird once," Julie says. "You don't get to see them very often."

"I saw a bald eagle in a zoo," someone else says. "It didn't look happy."

"Birds shouldn't be kept in cages," the guard says, without yelling. She actually smiles at us. "Well done, girls."

We go back to work. We clean up the mess that others have made and keep our eyes open for other fallen birds.

In Confrontation that evening, when the captain asks, "Does anyone have anything to report?" my hand is the first one in the air.

Front and center, I say, "This Prisoner Walters wishes to state her appreciation to her platoon members for helping to save the bird today." Then I turn sharply on my heels and go back to my seat.

No one says a word. I see the guards looking at each other, wondering how to respond.

Julie puts her hand up, and goes to the front. "This Prisoner Martin wishes to state she is grateful for Prisoner Sanchez's encouragement during the morning run."

Julie goes back to her seat. We start looking at each other, trying to guess what the guards will do.

Prisoner Blackstone marches up and thanks her teacher for helping her to learn long division. Prisoner Parry thanks the gardening crew for keeping the flowers blooming so nicely.

I see our Stripes guard put a hand over her mouth to hide a smile.

"Aren't you the cheerful little ladies, tonight?" the platoon captain snarls. "Anyone else?"

A fairly new girl goes to the front, pivots smartly, and says, "This Prisoner Heydon would like to thank her cubicle mate for teaching her how to keep her clothes tidy."

"Confrontation's over!" shouts the captain. We are sent out for twenty minutes of extra marching to fill up the time.

But there was no ratting. And, just this once, we have gotten away with it.

After lights out, I lie on my bed, listening to the other girls settling in around me. I think about the little bird, back in its home. I hope the mother bird hasn't rejected it.

Maybe I'll write to my family tomorrow. I'd like to tell them about the bird.

I close my eyes and try to get some sleep.

Four-thirty comes awfully early.

Dancing, With Beads

"Aren't you finished counting yet?"

Ramon paused in mid-count. Emilio, the Boss, had made him lose track. Ramon slid the little plastic bags of shaboo all together again on the table top and held his tongue. No one talked back to the Boss.

"You've made him go back to the beginning." A woman Ramon had never seen before was sitting on the sofa across the room, next to the Boss. "You've stressed the boy."

"Pay no attention to Mrs. Lozan," said Emilio. "She has an ulterior motive in keeping you healthy."

Ramon tuned out their voices and kept counting. He was running late. He didn't work *too* quickly, though. A mistake would only keep him there longer.

"One hundred," he said.

"That's what I counted, too," said Emilio, feeding bits of peeled mango to his small pet monkey. "So we are in agreement. One hundred packets of my precious shaboo, for which you will pay me now, and then resell for whatever you can get from those grubby little urchins who sell for you."

"That's right," said Ramon.

"Of course that's right. I didn't get to be the Shaboo King of Greater Manila by being wrong. You want my job?"

"No, Emilio." Ramon started packing the crystal meth into a flat bundle, which he would wear under his clothing undetected. He put aside a few packets for his trouser pockets, in case anyone came up to him on the street. He was becoming known as a shaboo man.

"Maybe the boy wants to earn some real money," Mrs. Lozan said.

That got Ramon's attention. He looked up at her from his packing. Mrs. Lozan was well dressed, with hair curled by a proper beauty salon and jewelry that looked expensive.

"I know of a rich Canadian who needs a kidney," she said. "You could get 50,000 pesos for lying around in a clean white hospital bed."

Ramon went back to packing his shaboo.

"You don't like that idea?" Mrs. Lozan asked. "You

think your kidney is too good to put into a Canadian? You have two kidneys. Nobody needs two."

Unconsciously, Ramon's fingers left the packets of meth and went to the small crucifix hanging around his neck. "God gave us two kidneys for a reason."

"God gave us tonsils, too, and tonsils are of no use to anyone."

"You can *have* my tonsils," Ramon said. It was slightly disrespectful to talk that way to a friend of the Boss, but Ramon said it with a smile so they would take it as a joke.

They laughed.

"Ramon doesn't want your Canadian's money. You want my shaboo empire, don't you, son?"

"No, Emilio."

"Well, what *do* you want?"

Ramon felt he had to say something, so he said, "Your tarsier."

Emilio laughed again and stroked the tiny brown monkey. With its great big eyes, and long fingers, it was a type of monkey only found in the Philippines. It was illegal for Filipinos or anyone else to keep them as pets, but the law was not something Emilio took very seriously.

"I can offer you girls, boys, marijuana, heroin, even a judge or a government official if that's where your appetite runs, but little BoBo stays with me." The Boss kissed the monkey's head. Ramon was sure the monkey would rather be back in the trees of Bohol.

"You seem to be in a hurry today, Ramon. Usually you like to take your time, ask about the business, try to pick my ample brain for the secrets of my success. Today, no questions, no dawdling."

"No, sir."

"I like the respect, but I'd rather have an answer. You look like a boy with something on his mind. The boys who work for me need to be empty-headed, except for their greed. And their fear of me."

"My mother is waiting for me," Ramon confessed.

"Outside my house?" Emilio started to stand up in alarm, sending the little monkey scampering up a shelf.

"No, no. At our house, in Pasay City."

"Is she going to cause me problems?"

"Oh no, sir. She…" Ramon had a hard time saying it because it was such an unusual, unexpected request. "She wants me to take her to the museum."

"The museum?" Mrs. Lozan sounded amused.

"Her and her friends."

"Manila is full of museums, boy," the Boss said. "There's the Aquarium, the Money Museum, the Air Force Museum. One day there will be a museum to me."

"The National Museum," Ramon told them. "My mother wants me to take her to the National Museum. I was there on a school trip five years ago, when I was eleven. She thinks I can get her in without trouble, and she insists it has to be today."

Ramon could tell that the Boss and his friend were already bored with his story.

"Just remember your priorities," Emilio said. "You are my employee first, your mother's son second. Now, go."

"Think about what I said," Mrs. Lozan added.

"*Don't* think about what she said," Emilio told him. "You can't sell shaboo from a hospital bed."

Ramon made one last check of the table, to make sure he hadn't left anything. He checked himself, too, to make sure he wasn't showing anything. The barong he was wearing had been one of his father's, who was killed in a traffic accident when Ramon was nine. It was too big for him still, and hung loosely from his shoulders. He hoped it would hide any bulge from the shaboo around his waist.

"And don't get caught leaving the house. If you do, the police will be the least of your worries."

The Boss said that every time Ramon left.

Ramon looked carefully in all directions, then stepped out of the house. He left by the back door, into an alley. The front door opened up to a green yard with flowers, enclosed by a high metal wall with a gate. The front door was not for the likes of Ramon.

The Boss worked out of a house in the Multinational Village, a neighborhood protected by a gate and private security guards. It was a part of Manila that was mainly for foreign nationals, mostly Chinese businessmen from Hong Kong but also Americans, British, Japanese, and others. The foreign teachers lived at their schools, and the diplomats lived in their embassy compounds. Filipinos went to the Multinational Village to clean, cook, cut grass, and look after the foreigners' children, but they didn't live there. The Boss was Filipino, which meant that the Boss had another boss.

Ramon caught a jeepney along Roxas Boulevard, too tied up in his thoughts to even notice Manila Bay. He switched jeepneys at San Rafael but had to walk from San Roque on. Jeepneys didn't travel to where Ramon lived. No vehicles did, not even fire trucks. A whole block of his neighborhood went up in flames once and fell into the river. The footpaths were not wide enough or strong enough to let a fire truck through.

Ramon could smell the river long before he got to it. By this stage in the dry season, the water left was more like sludge—clogged with garbage and sewage.

Ramon's community, like many others in Manila, extended over the river on stilts that got knocked away in the monsoons.

Thousands of people lived along this small piece of the riverbank, crowded into shanties made of scrap lumber, flattened cardboard boxes, and sheets of rusty corrugated tin. Some got hold of wooden beams stolen from construction sites, and some used clear plastic sheets or blue nylon tarps—whatever they could find.

There was some beauty, too, where people planted flowers in old tins or encouraged vines to grow so that big, colorful blooms covered the walls. Clothes, meticulously washed, the wrinkles smoothed out by hand, hung from hangers on nails inside and outside of the homes, like art that soaked up the sun and flapped when the breeze came up. When there was no breeze, clouds of mosquitoes made the neighborhood hum.

A stranger would get lost quickly. There were no clear pathways, no markings to indicate a narrow right-of-way between houses. Children without parents lived under bridges or in doorways and wandered into the river houses, bags of shoemaker's glue under their noses, looking for a bit of rice or plantain. They rummaged through the garbage, competing with the chickens and goats as they searched for something to eat.

There was commerce, too. A woman who owned a big pot cooked rice for women who didn't have one, in exchange for laundry or something else. Some sold oranges from boards perched on boxes. Others sold homemade hooch, brought in from the village stills and displayed alongside rosaries and secondhand clothes.

"Hey, Ramon, what's your hurry?" Enrique called out to him from his woodcarving shop.

Ramon stopped. "My mother is waiting," he said, but he couldn't resist pausing to look at what his friend was working on. "Is that St. Francis?" Enrique carved religious statues to sell to pilgrims and tourists.

"Do you like him?"

Ramon ran his thumb over the smooth wood of the saint's face. If he'd been able to stay in school, he would have trained to be a priest. Now, his mother was hoping one of his sisters would become a nun. Priests needed more than a grade-six education.

Maybe I could still do it, Ramon thought. *If I sell my shaboo for a lot of money, maybe I could go back to school.* Enrique was someone he could talk to about these things, not about shaboo—he didn't sell this close to home in case his mother found out—but about his wish for something more.

"A fancy woman asked to buy my kidney," Ramon said. "She promised me 50,000 pesos."

"That's a lot of money," Enrique said, working his hand-chisel slowly down a fold in St. Francis's robe.

"Yes, it is," agreed Ramon. "I've sold my blood before, but I only got thirty-five pesos for that." He remembered his waiting mother, said his good-byes, and hurried off. They'd continue their discussion later. It didn't seem right to sell a piece of himself. But 50,000 pesos!

Ramon ran the rest of the way to his house.

His mother and four of her friends were there, waiting.

"You're late," said his mother. "That boss of yours." He'd told his mother he worked as a houseboy in the Multicultural Village, washing cars and running errands.

"You could have gone without me," he said. "It's a public museum."

"They might not let us in. You've been there before. They'll remember you."

"That was five years ago. I was a child then. I'm a man now." It was the wrong thing to say in front of his mother's friends. They went into their cooing and cheek-pinching and isn't-he-a-cute-little-man routine. His mother put a stop to it.

"Let's go," she said.

"First I have to—"

"First you have to do nothing. You've kept us waiting long enough. We'll go now."

Ramon wanted to stash the shaboo up in the secret place in the rafters where he hid his money, but there was no point in arguing with his mother. He'd been alive for sixteen years and hadn't won an argument with her yet.

He started to take them to the jeepney stop, but his mother hailed a taxi instead. "We can't ride in a jeepney in our good clothes." Ramon saw then that all the ladies were in their best dresses, the ones they wore to mass.

"Ma, you don't have to dress up to go to the museum."

"Of course we do. We don't want those museum people to think we don't know how to act. Get in the taxi."

They drove up Taft Avenue, straight to Rizal Park and into Agrifina Circle, where the museum stood. They stopped in front of a magnificent white stone building—grand, with tall columns.

They all got out of the taxi, and the ladies carefully counted out the fare, adding a tip.

At the bottom of the steps, Ramon said, showing off a little, "This used to be the Congress building."

The women were a little slow in climbing the steps,

and at the entrance, they hesitated. Ramon's mother nudged his shoulder.

"This is why you are here," she said. "After all, you are a man." This started her friends laughing again, but timidly this time.

Ramon couldn't understand what the big deal was, although he could see that it was a big deal to his mother. He held the main door open for them and they walked into the museum.

Then he saw the look on his mother's face, and he understood.

She spent her whole life among garbage. She took whatever jobs she could find, usually piecework in factories, and she did piecework at home, too, on her days off. She never got to see the nice places in Manila. Ramon had gone on school tours of the city. His shaboo business took him to the Multinational Village and to other places his mother would never think of going. This trip to the museum was a very big deal, and he was sorry now that he'd been late.

"What do you want to see?" he asked.

"Show us everything," the women said. "Show us what you liked when you were here before."

Ramon played tour guide, leading them across the gleaming wood floors past spotless glass cabinets. He enjoyed himself. He even forgot for a while that he was a shaboo salesman with 100 packets of crystal meth strapped to his body. He became eleven years old again. He showed his mother and her friends the nature galleries, filled with the wonders of the Philippine rainforest. They saw the skull of the Tabon Man, the oldest human skull found in the area. And he showed them his favorite exhibit—the remains of the Spanish galleon that had sunk off the coast of the Philippines in the 1600s.

With every exhibit, the women would say, "My Maria would like that," or "My boys will enjoy this."

"I'm sorry, ladies, but the museum will soon be closing," a guard said, approaching the group with a little bow.

"So soon?" Ramon's mother asked. "It feels like we just got here."

"It's early closing today, madam." The guard's kind eyes and voice gave warmth to his formal manner.

"But the day after tomorrow?" one of his mother's friends asked. "Will it be open late the day after tomorrow?"

"Yes, it will be. Do you plan to return then?"

"Not us," said Ramon's mother, "but my son here will be back with all our children."

"I will?" asked Ramon. "Why?"

His mother took hold of Ramon's hand, but talked

to the guard. "We live in a slum down by the river. We make no apologies for this. We work hard and we do the best we can. Ramon, here, has had six years of school," she added proudly. "Our other children have not been so lucky." Then she said, "We've received notice that the day after tomorrow, bulldozers are coming to destroy our homes."

Ramon was shocked. "What? Why?"

"They say we are there illegally, and I guess we are. They say our shacks are fire traps, and that is true. They say the way we live is unhealthy, and they are right again. But they are still our homes. We don't want our children to have to watch their homes being destroyed. Ramon will bring them here and give them a good day, a day to remember when the days ahead are not so good."

They were all quiet then.

Ramon was stunned. They'd always lived by the river. Where would they go? Would they join the lost people living under bridges and along railway tracks? They deserved a place to live. He pictured the big houses in the Multinational Village. All that space. How many families could they hold?

"Wait here," the guard said. "You should have a good day, too. I must help close up the museum. But then I will show you a very special place."

Ramon left his mother and her friends and went in search of the men's restroom. He felt sure he was going to cry. He splashed water on his face and looked at his reflection. It was up to him now.

He put his hands on his waist and felt the drugs still strapped there. He would sell these packets quickly, then get more and sell them, too. He would find new places to sell, maybe at the rich private schools, where kids could afford to pay higher prices.

He'd lift his younger brothers and sisters out of the garbage, away from the stinking river. They'd go to sleep with full bellies in real beds, and they'd go on to become doctors and business managers, and lift the family up further to live in a house with a green lawn and a wall.

He'd find a way. He had to.

Ramon slipped his hand up under his barong and felt the skin on his belly, tight under his ribs. He tried to remember where his kidneys were. He felt for organs, pressing and trying to guess at shapes. Would there be just an empty space in him with one kidney gone? Would one side of his body feel heavier than the other side?

Would it hurt?

The museum was empty by the time he came out of the restroom. He went back to the place where he had left his mother. The guard was there.

"They are all in that back room," the guard said, pointing. "I think they are having a good time."

Ramon opened the door and looked inside. It was a large storage room for occasional exhibits. Music was playing—a waltz he guessed. The late afternoon sun came through the windows in long streams, like spotlights in a theatre. Racks of ballroom gowns and colorful folk costumes lined the walls. His mother and her friends were swaying to the music and holding the gowns against themselves—all ribbons and sequins, all shimmer and lace.

Ramon leaned against the doorway, watching these women who worked so hard every day and went hungry every night. Who loved their children and led lives without comfort. Who never had a holiday and were about to lose their homes. Ramon watched them waltz and saw their worries slip away, the youth come back into their faces.

He took a step forward, to join in their pleasure. But he stopped and held himself back. His turn would come later.

His eyes stung and he blinked hard as he watched the women, suddenly happy and beautiful. And in the center of them all was his mother. Her eyes were closed, her face was radiant, and she was dancing, with beads.

Prodigal

"You're coming with us," Kelly's mother told her.

"Dr. Beauchamp didn't say I had to. He said he didn't think it was necessary."

"Shannon needs to know she has our support. *All* our support. There will be other pageants."

"There will be other trips home from rehab, too," Kelly muttered.

"What did you say? Never mind. Get in the car. Your father's waiting for us."

"I said I'm not going. This is important to me. Why can't you pick her up tomorrow?"

"Because she's being discharged today." Kelly's mother held open the front door and pointed for Kelly to go through it. "We have a long drive ahead of us. Are you coming or not?"

"Not."

Her mother spun around angrily and left without saying good-bye or wishing her good luck. Kelly watched out the living-room window as her parents argued in the front seat, backed the car down the driveway, and drove away. They didn't even wave.

"Already it's starting," Kelly said to the empty house. "She's not even home yet, and already it's starting."

For sixty days, the house had been quiet. For two whole months the house had been free of Shannon's threats, thefts, tantrums, panic attacks, weeping, and lying on the couch, stinking, for days at a time. For sixty days, Kelly's parents had been relaxed. They'd slept through the night, made little jokes over morning coffee, and noticed that they had another daughter. Evenings were peaceful. Sometimes they rented a movie, watched it together, and talked about it afterward, bouncing reactions back and forth without fear of explosions. Most evenings, though, the television stayed off. If the stereo was on, it was tuned to quiet classical music. They sat together, the three of them, and read books, taking turns to fill the tea-pot, sometimes reading out loud the passages they found extraordinary.

Kelly believed that even the house around them had seemed relaxed.

For sixty days, the family played "Life Without

Shannon." It was such a wonderful game that Kelly could almost believe it was real. Not even the visit to the rehab center for family therapy could shake that feeling.

That's not my sister, Kelly said to herself when a nervous and strangely clean Shannon sat with them to talk about reentry. *That's some stranger we're being nice to, because we're a nice family.*

And soon it was all going to come to an end. Shannon was coming back. Money would disappear again from wallets, and jewelry would disappear from drawers. Acid rock would blast the walls. The living room would fill up with Shannon's friends, who didn't care that their beer cans left rings on the good furniture her parents had worked for and saved for, or if their cigarettes burned holes in the upholstery.

Her parents would fight, her mother would cry, her father would disappear for long hours into his basement workshop, emerging only to rage at Shannon when he found his tools missing—usually pawned. They'd hide the car keys from Shannon and forget where they put them. And they'd forget that they had two daughters.

Maybe there would be a car accident on the way back. An accident that wasn't their father's fault so he couldn't blame himself, one where her sister would be killed instantly and painlessly and her parents would walk away without a scratch. The only family therapy they'd have to go to would be to help them deal with their grief. They'd be gracious in receiving condolences and go back to their happy, quiet evenings. Everyone would be relieved, and there would be no need to say so. One problem solved, Shannon packed away in a box, put up on a shelf. Contained. Controlled. Quiet.

Kelly sighed. She was long past guilt, but there was no point in hoping.

A glance at the clock told her she'd better get busy. The Miss Firefighter Pageant started in two hours. She had things to do.

Straight hair was still in, but it had to be clean, brushed, and shiny. A close shave to the legs and new polish on her fingers—a light color, Faraway Pink. It was almost too young for her, but she thought the judges would like that. Miss Firefighter was a goodwill ambassador. They'd be put off by anything too mature looking.

"Keep sex out of it," Marla at the Sunny Side Shoppe had advised her. "Of course, it won't really be. But let them fool themselves that they're judging on the basis of freshness and youth."

A maiden in the forest. Everyone's dream of a granddaughter. Hope for the future. That was the look

Kelly was going for. Nothing smudged by rouge or knowledge, as wholesome as apple pie. Marla had helped her find the perfect dress, one she could wear for years if she didn't put on any weight.

Now all she had to concentrate on was her speech. She wouldn't mess up. She was a good student and had an excellent memory.

With no one to drive her, Kelly had to walk. The midsummer heat was intense, and she sweated as she carried her dress and shoes through the town. The cottagers had done their weekend shopping early. The whole town seemed to be wilting, except for the customers crowded into Dunkin' Donuts, gulping down Iced Lattes and soaking up the air conditioning. But they didn't linger on the streets. The weekenders still preferred their city shops. They didn't spend their money at the local fabric or shoe or gift stores. Even in the town's busiest season, shops were going out of business.

Kelly didn't like to walk past empty store fronts. They always made her sad. She could imagine people starting their new business, painting the walls, arranging the shelves, thinking this was *it*; they'd work hard, raise their kids, and build up a regular clientele. And they'd reap the rewards. She hated thinking about them packing up the store when they couldn't make a go of it.

It's not that I like the town so much, Kelly thought. *It's just that I don't like to see people disappointed.*

It all came back to Shannon. Because of Shannon, vacations had been canceled. Because of Shannon, Kelly's friends had drifted away. "Your sister's a druggy," they'd said, and Kelly had eaten lunch by herself. Because of Shannon, Kelly's whole family had become used to disappointment.

"If one person is addicted, the whole family is addicted," Shannon's social worker had told them. Well, Kelly wasn't addicted! *She* hadn't made those choices! *She* hadn't hung out with those people! *She* hadn't...

"Hey! Whoohoo!"

Local yahoos. Driving by and hanging out the windows, their whistles and catcalls interrupted Kelly's thoughts. Her anger had carried her all the way through town, and now she was walking along the country highway. The fire hall was just ahead.

Kelly checked her watch and tried not to think about her parents arriving at the rehab center. Maybe Shannon had a relapse and wouldn't be allowed to leave. Maybe she had run away and wouldn't be around for six months. Maybe her parents would get halfway to the center and turn around again. They'd walk into the fire hall and take seats in the audience because they realized they had already said their final good-bye to that bundle of rage and eye shadow they'd dropped off, screaming, two months ago.

In the tiny washroom-turned-dressing-room at the fire hall, it was all elbows and knees as the contestants got ready.

Kelly forced Shannon from her mind, and got caught up in the nervous giggling and the well-wishing: "You're going to win!" "No, *you're* going to win!" Kelly had known some of the girls since they'd all gone to the same school—Megan and Victoria and Valerie—but the others were from out of town, or maybe they went to the Catholic school. The Miss Firefighter Pageant was pretty silly, real small-town foolishness, but the winner would receive real prizes, and it was something to add to a college application. And it was something to do.

Finally, with the wooden stacking chairs in the fire hall filled with families, friends, and sponsors, the girls were ready to be paraded in. Kelly was third in line. The sash across her chest boldly read, Peter's Plumbing Supplies. They had paid her entry fee, which helped pay for the refreshments, and had given her a small grant toward her dress. Marla had stretched those twenty-five dollars as far as she could.

The stupid sash notwithstanding, Kelly thought she compared well with the other girls. Some were too showy, with too much of an attempt at glamour. This was small-town Ontario, not Vegas! Valerie's shimmering gold gown just looked silly under the Community Septic sash. It was her older sister's bridesmaid's dress, Kelly knew. From the looks of it, Valerie had spent her grant money on makeup.

It wasn't that Kelly cared so much about winning, but it would be embarrassing to lose. If she was going to be in it, she was going to win it.

Kelly lined up with the other six girls in the hallway outside the main part of the fire hall. The fire trucks were out in the parking lot.

"What if there's a fire?" Kelly heard one of the girls ask. "Will they still declare a winner?"

Fortunately, there was no time for anyone to answer such a lame question. A woman opened the door to the fire hall and stage-whispered, "Ready, girls? Walk tall, now, just as we rehearsed it." Someone changed the music in the CD player, the announcer did his thing, and into the hall they all walked.

They were supposed to do a slow, regal turn to the back of the hall, where the double garage doors were open to the hot August afternoon, then up through the center of the rows of spectators. They'd practiced a calm, measured walk; but Victoria, leading the pack, must have gotten spooked by all those relatives. She took off at a speed-walking pace. Kelly and the others had to keep up with her, or the line would have been hopelessly divided. They lined up at the front so quickly that the volunteer firefighter who was emceeing looked quite dizzy.

"Let's give them all a hand, ladies and gentlemen. Your 2008 Miss Firefighter contestants!"

Kelly scanned the crowd. She saw neighbors, folks from their church, a whole lot of very hot strangers fanning themselves with the souvenir program, but no one from her family. She began to relax a little. There was no way they could make it back in time, unless Shannon was packed and ready to roll without a tantrum or a fuss. Shannon never did anything without a tantrum or a fuss. It would be okay. Whatever happened at this silly pageant, it would belong to Kelly. Shannon wouldn't ruin it.

The emcee found his place on his little cue cards and invited the girls, one by one, to introduce themselves and say a few words about their sponsors. Kelly got through her little commercial for Peter's Plumbing Supplies with no problems. A clear voice, a smiling face, and lots of confidence without a touch of arrogance. Several girls fumbled. Megan, sponsored by Indoors Out, made a joke which got a big laugh, even though it wasn't all that funny. As far as Kelly could tell, Megan was her only real competition.

There weren't many opportunities to shine in a town like theirs. Local groups did what they could. They had sports teams, and the Optimist Club had a public-speaking contest. It wasn't quite rural enough for 4H and certainly not urban enough for an easy escape. Whatever the town offered, Kelly grabbed it. It helped to balance things out.

A hungover Shannon threw up in church one week, and Kelly read the scriptures the next. Shannon was arrested for breaking windows on the main street, and Kelly volunteered for the Community Clean-Up Weekend. Shannon wore blue spikes in her hair and black lipstick on her face, and Kelly sold daffodils for the Multiple Sclerosis Society. And so it went.

Kelly played the clarinet in the town band, chalked up the most books read in the Summer Kids' Read Festival at the library, collected badges in Girl Guides, and went on to the Provincials in the Spelling Bee. She couldn't make up for Shannon, but she could give her parents something else to talk to other parents about. "Kelly got a ninety-five on her math test" could balance out "Shannon didn't come home last night." "Kelly earned enough money babysitting to send herself to Girl Guide Camp," could almost make up for "Shannon stole my mother's wedding ring." Not that they ever talked about Shannon to their friends.

Phase Two of the competition was a fire safety quiz. Kelly had studied for this. The questions weren't hard, but a couple of the girls got them wrong. Megan got her answer half right, but she followed it up with a cute little grin aimed at the judges. Kelly kept her public smile on. She certainly wasn't going to lose to *that*!

Then they were at the third and final phase. Each girl had to give a two-minute speech about what the high office of Miss Firefighter would mean to her. Kelly had her speech down cold. Written, rewritten, and rehearsed in front of the mirror for sincerity, this is where she would sweep all the others out of the competition.

They'd drawn numbers backstage for the speaking order. Kelly was last. The fumblers fumbled. Megan got through her speech with no problem but also without saying anything. One girl spoke for barely thirty seconds then flopped down in her seat in tears.

The emcee decided to give the weeper a chance to catch her breath. He launched into the long list of thank-yous and into a description of the prizes. A $200 Canada Savings Bond. A back-to-school package from Buchwald's Office and Art Supplies. A year's membership at Murphy's Gym. A gift certificate for a family meal at Ribs and Fins. And the honor of riding on the big fire truck during the annual Riverfish Parade. Good prizes for a small town.

The weeper got to her feet again and this time made it all the way through her little speech. It wasn't very good, and she stumbled a lot, but she got through it, and everyone applauded as though she had single-handedly put out the Chicago Fire.

Then, at last it was Kelly's turn. The weeper now had a strong sentimental advantage, but overall Kelly thought she could still take it. She had the best steady performance. With this last speech, she'd nail it.

She had looked through the library's big book of quotations, wanting to start off with a quote from some famous person about the fire of ideas, or lighting the sparks of inspiration. The closest thing she could find was something Leon Trotsky had said, but she didn't think Trotsky was a good choice for Miss Firefighter. Instead, she went with the theme of community responsibility. Her speech was upbeat, articulate, and, she hoped, as rousing as a two-minute speech in a fire hall full of overheated relatives could ever be.

"We are all blessed in so many ways," she started out loud and clear, speaking to people, not just reciting. She smiled. She looked into their eyes. She connected.

And then she saw her family.

I will not fumble, she told herself. And she didn't. Focusing in on the row of judges, so that her eyes would not stray to the back of the room, she made it to the halfway mark.

"Why do we volunteer? To help others, certainly. To help ourselves, absolutely. We also volunteer to make a statement. This is the kind of community we want. This is the kind of country we want. This is the kind of world we want."

While she talked, she waited for the explosion from Shannon. It had come so many other times. Shannon throwing a tantrum during the spelling bee. Shannon dragged drunk from the high-school production of *Oklahoma* just when Kelly, as Ado Annie, was in the middle of singing "I Cain't Say No." Shannon stoned and making obscene gestures at the Christmas Eve Candlelight Service, where Kelly was acting the part of the Virgin Mary in the pageant. So many moments, big and small—holidays, family dinners, Saturday mornings. Shannon spoiled so many of them.

Kelly pushed those thoughts aside. Sixty seconds left in her speech. "It's not so much what we do as a community; it's how, as a community, we pull together to do good in all kinds of ways."

After a few strong words about fire safety, she wound it all up with her big finish—a recitation of the town motto.

When she heard the applause, Kelly knew that she had won. She got the feeling she always got when she was about to win something. She had won so many competitions that it was an easy feeling to recognize.

Now, she could dare to look at her sister's face. Whatever mess Shannon made now, it couldn't affect the outcome of the pageant.

But what she saw was not a mess, or a tantrum, or black lipstick. Her sister looked tired, and her hair wasn't that neat, but she was smiling and applauding. And what Kelly saw was that Shannon, too, knew that Kelly had won. And brimming on the edge of her smile was a faint expression of sadness that Kelly had never seen before.

It took only a few minutes for the judges to deliberate and put the Miss Firefighter sash over Kelly's shoulders. She gave her acceptance speech with only half her brain, and kept herself busy shaking hands, murmuring thank-you, and posing for photographs for the newspaper, taking care not to look in the direction of her family.

"So, like, if you die, I take over," said Megan, the runner-up, looking as though she'd be quite happy to push Kelly under a fire truck.

"I'll let you know if I start to feel weak," Kelly said. She left Megan to her second-place funk and headed to the buffet table, where the potato salad was on the verge of turning deadly in the heat. She skipped the food and reached for a drink.

"Congratulations," said Shannon, holding up a glass of punch. Her hand was trembling a little.

Kelly looked into her sister's eyes. There was no trace of meanness, no sign of mocking.

She didn't know what to do with this Shannon.

"I'm sorry," Shannon said, nudging the glass of punch at Kelly, urging her to take it.

She was just about to thank Shannon for not ruining the day when it hit her. How must it have been for Shannon all these years? Kelly, always perfect, always succeeding, getting all the praise.

What was it they kept saying at those meetings? One day at a time. Maybe this wasn't the same old day, Kelly thought as she pushed the Miss Firefighter crown from the Dollarama out of her eyes and accepted the glass of punch.

"It's good to see you, Shannon," she said.

And for that moment at least, she meant it.

Red Hero at Midnight

"**You're** not planning to try to sell that to the tourists, are you?"

Liko was startled out of the drawing he was doing of the statue of Damdin Sukhbataar, the hero of the Mongolian Revolution. He'd been lost in the drawing, but the officer's shadow was a curse. His fingers suddenly cramped with cold.

"Look at me when I speak to you."

Liko made himself look at Officer Zorig and was reminded, as always, of the camel that his father kept tethered outside the family's yurt long, long ago.

"I will not try to sell it."

Still, the policeman did not go away. "You wouldn't be able to find a buyer anyway. All you've done is draw the horse's ass over and over. What kind of a drawing is that?"

Liko looked up at the statue of the hero proudly astride his horse. If there had been a point to it, Liko would have explained that he had positioned himself at this very spot so he could draw the hindquarters of the horse over and over, to get closer to drawing them properly. But there was no point. With Officer Zorig, there were only two choices: silence or agreement. Liko had already agreed. Now he would be silent.

Officer Zorig reached down with his big, gloved hand, grabbed the drawing, and crumpled it up in front of Liko's face.

"Get out of my square," he ordered.

Liko ran, dropping in his haste the piece of cardboard he was using as a lap-desk but managing to hold tight to his pencil. He kept running all the way out of Sukhbataar Square, not because he was scared of Officer Zorig—although he was—but because he was late to meet Dimka and the others.

The streets of Ulan Bataar were filling up with people eager to get home to their suppers. Liko moved against the crowd, bumping into people, getting swatted by some, then ducking across empty lots and alleys. He knew the city well. He lived inside it every single day.

Then, in the scrap land behind a pizza house, he spotted them.

Dimka, at fifteen, was only a year older than Liko but was much taller and easy to spot. The rest of the group stood together by the sewer opening, reviewing their plans, getting ready. Panting, Liko joined them.

"We thought you'd been nabbed," Dimka said. "There's no other reason for being late."

"It got dark faster than I thought," Liko said. He kept his drawing to himself. The others knew he drew—how could they not, they lived on top of each other—but drawing was not a good reason to miss work. "I got stopped by Zorig." *That* was a good reason.

Dimka spat on the cobblestones at the mention of the policeman's name. Ajii, one of the younger boys, tried to do the same; but he spat into the wind so the effect wasn't the same. If Dimka saw, he pretended not to, so Liko followed his example.

"Does everybody know what to do?" Dimka asked. "Are there any questions?"

Everyone was ready. There were seven kids in their group, their family, now. A few at a time, they left the wasteland and took up their spots in the streets and alleys, all close to Dimka as he settled down on a broken cement block on the sidewalk. Liko, just behind him in the alley, was the closest, but not by much. Everyone was just a leap away.

Within moments, Dimka looked so settled on his block he could have been there all day. Liko admired Dimka's ability to blend in with the scenery so that people passing by took no notice. They couldn't see beneath the layers of Dimka's rags to his muscles, tense and ready to jump.

Liko kept his eyes on Dimka. For a long while, Dimka didn't move. The people passing by were Mongolians or Chinese. Either they didn't have much money or they were likely to go to the police if they were robbed. Dimka, Liko knew, was waiting.

A slight nod, and Liko got ready to spring. Dimka shuffled to his feet, looking stoned and sleepy. Into Liko's field of vision came a traveler, a man from either Europe or America, with a big pack on his back and a small one around his belly. He was wearing a warm, Western-style jacket.

"Money?" Dimka asked in English. "Food? Hungry."

Dimka had taught their whole family to say these words.

The traveler stopped and unzipped a pocket on the side of his jacket.

In the next instant, they were upon him. Six kids leapt out of their hiding places and grabbed whatever they could.

It took the traveler nearly a full minute to understand what was happening.

"Smile," Dimka had told them. "Smile so they will be confused."

So they smiled, and they sang, and they chirped out their English words as they pawed and distracted the stranger. While he fended off an attack from the front, Liko's penknife sliced through his backpack straps.

The children pulled the traveler into the darkness of the alley, where the sounds would be muffled and anyone passing by would think it was just the sound of drunks fighting.

The backpack and belly pack were snatched away and carried off by kids running in different directions. Dimka and Liko, still without a prize, stayed behind to give the others time to get away. Liko wanted the coat.

The man was really fighting them now, but Dimka was strong—he did chin-ups on the pipes in the sewer—and there were two of them attacking and backing off. It was like a dance, they moved so well together.

Dimka made a final grab at the traveler's coat, got it, and tossed it to Liko. Then they ran away from the street and down the alley. When they got to the end of the alley, they split into different directions. It was always safer to split up.

Liko, clutching the coat, was half a block away when he heard the sirens, coming closer then stopping behind him. *Keep running*, he told himself. But he heard a car door slam and turned around in spite of himself.

There was just enough twilight to see Officer Zorig knock Dimka to the ground.

Liko ducked behind a garbage can, his knees jamming into some broken glass. He watched his friend, the family's leader, being tossed into the back of the police car and taken away. It took every bit of self-control Liko had not to leap out and try to rescue his friend, especially when he heard Dimka crying out in pain from the blows Zorig was landing on him.

Liko stayed in his hiding spot until the police car drove away. Then he was alone.

The enormity of what had just happened was clear. He, Liko, was next in line to lead the family. It was only temporary, of course—one of his first jobs would be to get Dimka out of jail—but for now, he was the leader. And he had to get home. He put his thin arms into the big, warm coat and headed off.

He was actually calm now, crossing yards and alleys, using pathways that were hidden from most of the city. When he came to the sewer grate he was looking for, he opened it up and stepped inside.

Liko had to push up the sleeves of his new coat so his hands would be free to grip the metal ladder pinned to the side of the hole. He felt the warmth of the steam pipes rise up from below.

The others were waiting for him in the alcove, not far from the opening to the tunnel. Dimka had fixed it up nicely for everyone. Flattened cardboard boxes lined the concrete walls and floor, and there were blankets, too—nearly one for each of them.

"Where's Dimka?" Ajii asked. He was about ten, Liko thought. Ajii himself didn't know how old he was.

Liko didn't answer right away. He was the leader now. He could answer questions when he felt like it.

He saw that they were waiting for Dimka before they opened the bags they stole. That was Dimka's rule: share everything so everyone gets what they need. Liko nodded his approval and said, "Zorig got him."

There was silence, then Halta, the older girl, said, "You didn't rescue him?"

We were separated, Liko started to say. *I couldn't reach him. Zorig would have nabbed me, too.* But a leader shouldn't have to explain.

"I'll get Dimka back," he said.

"How?"

"You'll know my plan when I choose to tell you."

"That's not how Dimka would do it," said Nara, the only other girl in the group. She was roughly the same age as Ajii. "He'd say, 'Do any of you have any ideas?'"

"My plan is to hear ideas later," said Liko. "We'll open the bags now."

They all wanted to see what was in the bags, so they got busy opening zippers and straps.

Their alcove was lit by several candle stumps set up along the edges. They got the candles out of hotel dumpsters. It was bad when they ran out. The darkness was total, and the little ones got scared. Sometimes there was too much steam in the tunnels to get the candles to light.

The candles were burning now, and they gave just enough light to show what the bags contained. The children sat in a semicircle on their bed of cardboard and blankets and dumped the contents of the bags into the center.

"We're rich," said Stephan. He and Sukhe were both thirteen. They called themselves brothers and were never apart.

The big backpack held sweaters, shirts, underwear (which were held up and laughed at), and trousers. There was food, too: packets of dry soup that could be mixed with the hot water they got from an underground tap, bags of nuts and dried fruit, and bars of chocolate.

Food was good to have, but it was also dangerous. Food brought rats. Halta wrapped it up as best she could when they had some, but rats could smell through anything.

"What about the smaller bag?" Liko asked when Stephan shook the backpack upside down to show there was nothing more inside.

The belly pack and the wallet produced some Mongolian money, some foreign money, credit cards, and a passport. Liko divided up the Mongolian money. There wasn't much. Each kid received a share so that they could buy food on the street instead of having to steal it. The biggest share went to Halta. She kept a stash of money hidden so that they could eat when things went bad. The coming winter would mean fewer tourists, and the deep, dark cold would make everything harder. Already Nara had a bad cough; soon they'd all end up with it. If there was extra money, they could buy medicine.

"Who will deal with these?" Halta asked, nodding to the passport and the foreign money. "Who will take them to Mr. Kozak?"

"I will," Liko said.

"But that's Dimka's job," Sukhe said.

"I'll do it," said Liko. "I know what to do." The others stared like they didn't believe him. "I'll do it," Liko said again. "Mr. Kozak will want them. He won't care who brings them."

"He'll cheat you," said Halta.

"He cheats Dimka, too," said Liko.

Nara was feeling the bottom of the backpack and looking inside it. "There's something in here, but there's nothing in here," she said.

Liko took the bag from her. There *was* something in the bottom. He made some cuts with his penknife, tugged and pulled with his fingers, and brought out a thick plastic bag full of white powder. He tossed it on the blanket so they could all see it.

"What is it?" Ajii asked.

"Drugs," said Halta.

Nara coughed. "For me?"

"For no one," said Halta. "They aren't the kind of drugs that will help you. The man is a smuggler. I'm glad we robbed him." She slapped away Sukhe's hand as he reached for the bag, and handed it back to Liko. "Take this with you to Mr. Kozak. Maybe he'd buy it, too."

Liko tucked the passport, credit cards, and currency away in his pockets. He tried to find a place to carry the drugs, but none of his pockets were big enough to hide the packet.

"Maybe I'll ask Mr. Kozak about it first," he said. "See if he's interested."

He left the alcove and moved down the sewer to his secret place. There was no light here, but Liko counted his steps and used his hand along the cement wall as a guide. He was used to the scuttling of rats. Used to it but didn't like it.

He came to a spot where the narrow ledge above his head widened to a shelf that continued into a hollow behind the wall. He reached up and took down a tin that had once held chocolates but now held his memories—a photo of his parents, taken before they got the fever and died, some fleece from one of the family's sheep, a small camel his father carved out of wood, and a bell that had hung in the doorway of their yurt and jingled whenever someone went in or out. He put the drugs behind the wall, then put the tin back in its place.

It was always hard going back out into the cold after being in the warm, damp sewers. The veil of moisture on his skin made the cold that much worse. In the middle of winter his face would feel like it was freezing solid.

Liko knew the way to Mr. Kozak's shop. He'd gone there with Dimka, but only as a lookout. He'd never done the negotiating.

He moved quickly through the dark parts of the city, keeping to the shadows until he got to Brezhnev's Gift, the neighborhood dense with ugly apartment buildings built by the Soviets back when they were investing in Mongolia. Mr. Kozak's shop was little more than a closet underneath a bare lightbulb. He sold candy and cigarettes, but his biggest earnings came from dealing in stolen goods.

Liko stopped at the corner he always stayed at when he played lookout for Dimka.

"Mr. Kozak doesn't like children," Dimka once told him. "I don't feel good in there. I know he's cheating me, but it's more than that. I think he's dangerous." Dimka felt better with Liko watching out.

The streets were almost completely dark. Many of the streetlights didn't work, making the light from Mr. Kozak's shop look that much brighter. Liko could see Mr. Kozak's big head, his powerful arms leaning on the counter as he read a newspaper. No one else was in the shop, and no one was approaching. There would be no better time.

Liko didn't think about it too much. Thinking only made him more afraid. He took a deep breath and stepped out into the street.

He was yanked back into the shadows.

"Not so fast, sewer rat."

Officer Zorig's voice made Liko's heart stop.

The policeman spun him around, keeping a firm grip on his arm. Next to the cop stood the traveler, now in a warm policeman's coat.

"You have something that doesn't belong to you," Zorig said.

Liko's face hit the brick wall as he was flattened against it and searched. Zorig found the cash and the credit cards, and handed them back to the traveler. The new coat was stripped from Liko's back and he was pushed to the ground.

"Where is it?" Zorig demanded, kicking as he yelled. "Where is it?"

Liko curled into a ball and tried to protect himself.

"That won't get us what we want," the traveler said in Mongolian. He pulled Liko to his feet and wrapped the coat around Liko's shoulders. "Keep the coat," he said. "I can buy another coat. I may even keep this one the police loaned me." He tried to dust Liko off, but the streets were damp and the grime stuck. "I've done a favor for you, now you do a favor for me. Where is the backpack?"

Liko's head was racing. What would Dimka do?

"I want my friend out of jail," he said. "Fair exchange."

He saw Zorig's hand go up and ducked just in time for Zorig to slam the wall instead of him. Zorig cursed and regained his dignity by picking Liko up and dragging him around the corner, where the police car sat. Then the officer hurled Liko into the back of the car.

Liko was *not* going to go to jail quietly. He yelled and screamed and banged his feet against the window, trying to break the glass. Zorig came roaring up to the car but was stopped by the traveler. They talked for a moment, then the traveler stuck his head in the front door.

Liko stopped yelling. "My friend?"

"Are you hungry?" The traveler motioned to Officer Zorig to take the driver's seat. Liko almost laughed at the look on Zorig's face, but the policeman got behind the wheel.

"I think this boy's hungry," said the traveler. "I think his tongue will loosen with a bowl of noodles."

"Noodles?" snarled Zorig.

"Let's all have some noodles. Noodles and conversation."

Officer Zorig channeled his anger into his driving, making pedestrians run and other cars swerve. He pulled up so suddenly in front of a noodle shop that Liko was afraid they'd drive right through the window.

Zorig kept a firm grip on Liko as they went into the restaurant. The windows were foggy with steam from the hot noodles. Zorig shoved Liko into a booth and sat down beside him so that the boy couldn't run away.

No one spoke except the traveler, who ordered noodles and chicken for the three of them. When the food came, Liko ate. He would have been a fool not to.

"Here's what we'll do," the traveler said. Neither he nor the policeman was eating noodles. Liko kept an eye on their bowls as he ate. Maybe he could eat their food, too.

"Here's what we're going to do," the traveler repeated. "We're going to release your friend." Zorig made a noise but held his tongue. "We're also going to help you out with other things—some gloves, some socks. I've heard about you sewer kids. You tell me what you need, and if it's reasonable, we'll get it for you."

"You're rewarding these thieves," Zorig muttered.

"We're doing business," the traveler corrected and pushed his bowl over closer to Liko. Zorig moved his bowl out of reach. "Think about what you want."

Liko shoveled noodles into his mouth and thought hard. "Light," he said. "Some kind of light that won't go out. Something to keep the damp off the blankets. And more blankets." He could see the little alcove in his head as he spoke. "Food and some way of keeping the rats out of the food. And medicine for coughs. And warm clothes. And soap," he added, thinking of one of Halta's wishes.

The traveler wrote down his list. "Anything else?"

Liko had a wish, but was shy about saying it in front of Officer Zorig. Then, figuring he had nothing to lose by asking, he said, "I want things to draw with, like artists use."

Officer Zorig laughed. "Why not a color TV?" he sneered. "Why not a marble bathtub?"

The traveler ignored him. "Do you have my property?" he asked Liko. The boy nodded. "Where is it?"

"It's safe."

"It's probably hidden down one of those rat holes he lives in," said Zorig.

"It's safe," Liko repeated.

"Let's go get it," said the traveler.

"No," said Liko. "I'll bring it to you." He didn't want them anywhere near his family.

"You don't control things here!" said Zorig.

"Where and when?" asked the traveler.

"Midnight," Liko said. "Up at the Zaisan Memorial."

"Of all the crazy...!"

"Fine," said the traveler.

Liko swallowed the last of the noodles. Zorig got up from his seat. As Liko slid past him, Zorig said, "If you screw with us, your friend will meet with an accident in jail, and I will personally flood the sewer with poison gas to kill you and your other rat friends!"

He let Liko go. Liko ran out of the restaurant and didn't look back.

All the way to the sewer entrance, he worried that the rats had somehow gotten into the plastic bag, or that it had been found by a rival family. His heart was beating fast as he climbed down into the sewer and felt his way along the tunnel until he came to the hiding place. The bag was still there.

He tucked it into the top of his trousers and headed back up to the street. There were still a couple of hours until midnight, but the memorial was at the south end of the city, and up a steep flight of stairs. He started out.

Ulan Bataar sat in a bowl surrounded by the Bogd Khan Mountains. All around the city, up above the buildings and the traffic noises, fires could be seen burning outside the yurt camps of the nomads and sheepherders, like an extra layer of stars.

Liko found the bottom of the staircase and began to climb. High above, spotlights shone on the giant white stone soldiers of the memorial.

It was a long climb up, three hundred steps. But it was a shorter trip than taking the road. Liko had to stop frequently to ease the ache in his legs, but he made it to the top. He sat at the foot of the massive soldier and let the cold air rush inside his jacket.

He took the packet of drugs from the top of his trousers and held it, squishing the bag full of powder and wondering what would come next.

Before long, he heard a car pull up behind him. The doors opened and shut, and Liko heard footsteps.

A hand reached down and took the packet of drugs away from Liko. Officer Zorig sat down beside him.

"You must think you're very smart," Zorig said. "You're not smart. You're lucky. Of course, I could still pick you up and throw you off the mountain. You know that, don't you? But I won't, but not because I like you."

The traveler dumped a pile of blankets and things to the ground, and went back to the police car for another load.

"You're going to keep working for me," Officer Zorig said. "You'll follow who I tell you to follow, you'll carry what I tell you to carry, and you'll give me a first look at everything you steal."

The traveler dropped another load onto the pavement.

Liko looked out over the city and across that to the mountains. He remembered something his father had told him. "Ulaan Bataar means Red Hero," he said.

Zorig snorted and got to his feet. "There are no heroes," he said. "Here's your friend. He works for me now, too." He went back to the car. The doors slammed, and the car drove back down the hill.

Liko stood and faced Dimka. "I didn't think they'd actually let you go," he said. "Are you all right?"

Dimka nodded, and touched his foot to the pile of goods. "You bargained well," he said.

"Except now we have to work for Zorig," said Liko.

"That's tomorrow's worry," said Dimka.

The two boys loaded themselves up with blankets and bundles, and headed down the stairs.

They had family waiting.

Another Night in Disneyland

Laura opened the curtains of the Witlaws' living room and looked out across the cul-de-sac.

Not that there was anything to see, just another house exactly like the one she was babysitting in—white clapboard with high, steep rooftops. All the homes looked the same in this little circle of Hay River, Northwest Territories.

The only splash of color under the streetlights came from the deep red bear-proof garbage bins parked out by the Canada Post boxes. Laura wondered why there were boxes, not mail delivery to each house, but she didn't wonder too much. She tried not to think about anything too deeply if it was associated with Hay River, including why this weird little oval of weird little houses was called Disneyland. Thinking about anything Hay Riverish reminded her of how angry she was at being hauled up here by her mother, who was on a three-year nursing contract. That much anger was too hard to live with, especially when there was nothing she could do to fix it.

Two guys from her high school appeared in the Disneyland circle. They leaned against the bear boxes as if hanging around garbage was the most natural thing to do on a Saturday night. They were talking. Laura couldn't hear their words, but from their body language, they seemed to be just passing the time, trying to look like they weren't up to anything.

Laura turned off the living-room lamp so she could watch them without being noticed. The Witlaws had smashed in their TV, and Laura's library book turned out to be a dud. Watching the guys was something to do.

Standing around looking casual didn't amuse the guys for long, so they switched to climbing onto the garbage bins and jumping off again. That ended when a police car came by.

Are you boys damaging those bins? Laura imagined she could hear the officer say.

No, Officer, the boys appeared to be saying.

"Well, stay off them anyway. You want bears in our streets?" Laura muttered as the officer made one more comment before driving away.

The boys reserved their obscene gestures for when

the police car was out of sight. They kicked at the bins in defiance but stayed off them. Then they checked the mailboxes, but they were all locked.

Nothing happened for a while, and Laura was about to give her book another try when a taxi pulled up to the bins. The streetlight caught the driver's face. It was Hakim, the guy from the Sudan. She'd ridden in his cab a few times. He told her he was in Hay River to escape the diamond-mine-boom drug addicts and drunks he'd driven around in Yellowknife. Laura wondered how much farther north he'd have to go. Maybe all the way up, over the Pole, and down the other side until he got back to Khartoum, where he started out. It gave Laura some comfort that there was at least one person in Hay River who was farther from home than she was.

A man got out of the back of the cab and talked to the boys. Laura saw Hakim turn his face away, probably so he didn't have to witness what the man was doing. Then, right out in the open, the exchange was done. Laura didn't see what was given for what, but something was given for something. It didn't take much imagination. After all, she was fourteen and knew a thing or two about the world.

The man got back in his cab, Hakim stepped on the gas, and the boys wandered away to swallow, inhale, or inject whatever it was they now had to swallow, inhale, or inject. Disneyland was quiet again. Entertainment done, Laura dropped the curtain and looked around.

The house was filthy. When she first started baby-sitting for the Witlaws, she used to help them out —putting in a load of the children's laundry, wiping off tables, doing dishes, sweeping floors. It used to worry her, the things she didn't have time to get done. But the Witlaws didn't pay extra for the cleaning, and worse still, they didn't even seem to notice.

Except for the time Mrs. Witlaw came home early, caught Laura washing the kitchen floor, and yelled, "So you think I'm not a good mother? What would you know about it? I love my kids!"

So now Laura washed only enough dishes to feed the kids off clean plates, and she cleared just enough space in the living room to sit without touching garbage.

To eat up a few more minutes, Laura climbed the stairs to check on the kids. The children—Ashley, four, and Ethan, two—were sound asleep. Laura pulled the covers back up over Ashley and tucked the little boy's leg back under the blanket. The room smelled strongly of urine. She doubted the sheets had been washed in weeks.

I'm getting to be just like my mother, Laura realized in horror. But really, cleaning wasn't that big of a job. What was wrong with these people?

At least they paid, and in advance, too, before they went out. Otherwise, Laura would have told them to find another sitter.

"Probably they wouldn't," she muttered. "Probably they'd go off to the bar and leave the kids home alone."

She leaned down to pick up a pile of dirty clothes to put in the washer, then stopped herself. She had decided not to do that anymore. But kids need clean clothes, and for now, wasn't she responsible for these kids? If they didn't have clean clothes to wear tomorrow, wouldn't that be partly her fault?

Laura was tired and bored and grumpy, and this philosophical argument did not help her mood. In the end, to shut herself up, she took the clothes down to the laundry room and shoved them in the washing machine without bothering to separate the colors. She put her blinders on as she stepped back through the disgusting kitchen, her feet crunching and sticking to the floor.

She was going to go back to her book when she saw car headlights through the front-door window. Standing on her tiptoes, she looked out just as the car doors banged and the shouting began.

The Witlaws were back.

They were back early, and they were fighting.

Usually they showed up after the bars had closed, driving themselves—where were the police?—and both too wasted to do much beyond stumble up the front steps and collapse into a stinking, snoring heap in the living room while Laura let herself out.

But it was barely midnight, and they were fighting, and that meant trouble. It sure did the last time, when they screamed and threw things while Laura and the children scrambled to stay out of their way.

Laura stood at the closed door, frozen in panic until the yelling reached the other side of the door and the handle turned. Then her legs sprang into action, and she leapt up the stairs and into the children's room. She closed the door, then grabbed the toy box and dragged it in front of the door.

The yelling flew through the house, up the stairs, and into the ears of the children. Ethan started to cry. Ashley sat up in her bed, silent, her eyes wide.

Laura picked up Ethan and jiggled him to get him to shush. She sat beside Ashley on the bed, trying to think of something reassuring to say. In the absence of that, she sang a little song about a bear that her own mother had sung to her.

Now they could hear the sounds of smashing and banging on top of the yelling. Laura made a decision.

"Let's play a game," she said, keeping her voice light. "Let's play hide-and-seek."

She pulled the blanket off Ethan's bed. She helped

Ashley into her slippers, threw a sweater over the little girl's nightgown, and grabbed a blanket for her, too.

With Ethan in one arm, Laura gripped Ashley's hand and used her foot to slide the toy box. She waited at the bedroom door until she could tell from the sound that the fight had moved to the kitchen at the back of the house.

"Quick like a bunny," Laura said. Another Mom moment, but there wasn't time to worry about that. Down the stairs and out the front door Laura flew with the kids, grateful it wasn't the dead of winter. She hadn't experienced a Hay River winter yet, but it was waiting for her, a nightmare she wouldn't be able to avoid.

The other houses were dark. Maybe she could have banged on any door at random and been taken in. You're supposed to be able to do that in small towns. But Laura had only been in Hay River a couple of months and had kept her head down. She wasn't intending to stay here long enough to get to know anyone; and that left her at midnight, in Disneyland, with two scared kids and a dead end of closed doors.

Home was an apartment in the town's one and only high-rise, a fair walk from Disneyland; but there was no point in sticking around the circle, hoping Hakim would come by with another drug dealer to make a sale.

"It's nighttime," Ashley said.

"A good time for a walk," Laura said. She could still hear the yelling in the house behind them, so she started walking quickly. Time to get away from the Witlaws. Ashley shuffled along beside her on little legs and slippered feet. In frustration, Laura picked her up and ran as far as she could with her arms full of children and her face full of smelly blankets. It wasn't far, but at least it was away. She got them around a corner and out of sight of the house before putting Ashley back down on the sidewalk.

Not many cars went by, but some did. No one stopped to see why a teenaged girl was out wandering around after midnight with two small children.

Then someone slowed down his car and started in with the obscene remarks. Sickened, Laura pulled Ashley close and headed toward the nearest house. The jerk, laughing, drove away.

"What did he mean?" Ashley asked.

"He was just saying it's a nice night," Laura said.

"I'm cold," Ashley said, "and tired." Ethan started to whimper.

Laura heard a car slow down behind them. Thinking it was the jerk again, she spun around and yelled, "Just leave us alone!"

"Can't do that," the driver said. But it was a woman's voice, not a man's. The car pulled up closer.

"Looks like you've put as much thought into this kidnapping as you did into your last essay."

"Ms. Greer!" Laura was stunned and relieved to see her history teacher. "I'm not kidnapping. I'm babysitting."

Ms. Greer got out of the car and picked up Ashley. "Let's get you into a nice warm car," she said. They strapped the kids into the back seat, Ms. Greer tsk-tsking about not having proper car seats. After tucking blankets around the little ones, Laura and Ms. Greer got in the front.

"These are the Witlaw children?" Ms. Greer asked. Laura nodded.

"And if they *could* be in bed, they would be in bed. Am I right?"

"The Witlaws are having a bad night," Laura said.

"Drunk?" Ms. Greer saw Laura hesitate. "Babysitters are not bound by rules of confidentiality like lawyers or doctors. What's your plan?"

"Take them home with me, I guess. It happened pretty fast. I didn't have time to come up with a plan."

Ms. Greer turned and looked at the children. Ethan was already asleep, and Ashley was sucking her thumb, her eyes starting to close. "They've had a horrible time of it," she said.

"I know. Poor kids. You should see the filth they live in."

"I meant the parents," said Ms. Greer. "They've had a horrible time."

"They're just horrible people. This whole place is horrible." Laura kicked at the inside of the car door. "People make choices, don't they? Bad things happen all the time, but not everybody acts like the Witlaws. Look at me. I've lost my whole life, and I'm not drinking and making a mess of things."

"Yes, look at you." Ms. Greer took her cell phone out of her purse, but just held it in her hand, staring at it.

Laura kept talking and kicking. "I had friends back in Toronto! There were things to do. Going to the movies, swimming at the pool, shopping at the mall."

Ms. Greer put her hand on Laura's leg to stop the kicking. "I'm trying to think."

Laura shut up. *I hate this place*, she thought for the millionth time.

Ms. Greer let out a deep breath, then punched some numbers into the phone. "Paul? It's Betty. The Witlaws are at it again. Yeah, bad. You'd better get over there. I have the children." She put the phone back in her bag. "Sorry, my friend, but this has to stop," she said to herself.

Then she looked up and turned to Laura. "What were you saying? Oh, yes. You hate it here, and everyone is horrible."

The way Ms. Greer said it made Laura feel almost embarrassed, but she kept it up. "Well, it is, and they are. Maybe you don't think so because this is all you know, but I'm from Toronto, and—"

"You shouldn't make assumptions, you know—they're as sloppy as your school work."

Laura could have punched her. "I just meant that I had a good life back there. I had friends. We were going to audition for commercials. You can do that in Toronto and make real money, not just babysitting money. And now I'm stuck here, where there's nothing. Nothing! I go to the library, and when I come out, I look one way down the street, then turn and look the other way, and it doesn't matter where I go because they both end up nowhere!"

Ms. Greer started driving.

"My house is the other way," Laura said when the car turned left instead of right. Ms. Greer kept silent. They drove to the edge of town, where Ms. Greer stopped the car and turned off the motor.

"Over there is the Greyhound station," she said. "Down the road is the airport, and the train station isn't far, either. Hay River isn't a dead end. There are ways out of town."

Laura chewed her thumbnail in frustration. "My mother's job is here. She likes it here. I've got no choice. I have to stay."

"There must be someone in the south who could look after you until you finish high school," Mrs. Greer said. "Some sort of relative."

Laura didn't reply.

"Isn't there?" pressed Ms. Greer. "Some sort of relative?"

"My aunt is in Winnipeg," Laura admitted. Thinking of her dad's sister, whose offer was only given because she knew it wouldn't be accepted, made the inside of Laura's chest go cold.

"So that's one choice," Ms. Greer said. "Staying here is another. That's two choices already, and we've only started talking."

"They're rotten choices," Laura said.

"But they're still choices. Choose one of them, or think of others. But you should think about dropping the whining routine. It got old pretty fast around here, you know."

Laura was glad the darkness hid her face. "Nobody even notices me."

"Of course you're noticed. You're noticed for being a whiner, for walking around in a dark cloud of misery. And for what? For getting the opportunity to live in a beautiful place that very few people will ever have the chance to see? You don't really want people to hate you, do you? You don't want everyone counting down the days until they're finally rid of you."

Laura's mouth dropped open. "You...you're not... supposed to talk to me like that. You're my teacher."

"Then here's a lesson. What's that?" She pointed out the front window of the car. The sky was dancing.

Laura knew what it was. She had purposely avoided looking up at the sky when her mother was around. If she showed interest in anything, even the Northern Lights, her mother would take it as a sign that she'd agreed to stay.

"The Inuit call them Sky Spirits," Ms. Greer said. "The legend is that the lights are torches the Sky Spirits carry when they take the newly dead across the abyss and into the land of joy and plenty."

Laura looked, in spite of herself, at the shifting shades and colors.

"There's a narrow bridge over the abyss," Ms. Greer continued. "Without the Sky Spirits, the dead might never get across it. They might fall into the abyss and be lost. And then who would we talk to when we are all alone?"

"Stories," Laura said, but the word came out of her without the sneer she'd intended.

"Stories," agreed Ms. Greer. "That's really all we leave behind us. Good stories and bad stories. Sometimes, we get to choose." She turned the key in the motor. "The police should have them rounded up by now. I don't want the children to see their parents arrested."

Red flashing lights spun around the circle when Ms. Greer rolled into Disneyland. "Watch the kids," she said as she stepped out of the car. Ashley and Ethan were sound asleep. Laura rolled her window down so she could hear.

"You'll hold them for the night?" Ms. Greer asked the officer.

"Drunk and disorderly. Causing a disturbance. That should hold them until we can get them into detox."

"Thanks, Paul," Ms. Greer said. She bent low over the police car to say a few words to the Witlaws. They were sitting in the back seat, subdued, as if the air had been let out of them. Laura couldn't hear the words, but they didn't sound angry.

The police car drove away. Ms. Greer helped Laura carry the children into the house, and Laura tucked them back into bed.

"I've called a taxi for you," Ms. Greer said, when Laura met up with her in the kitchen. Her history teacher was already up to her elbows in soap suds. "I'll stay with the kids."

"You're cleaning up?" Laura asked. "You don't have to," she said, even though as she said it, she knew that wasn't the point.

"Everybody deserves a fresh start," Ms. Greer said. "You'd better gather up your things."

Laura found her library book and her jacket and got herself ready to go. She stood at the window and waited.

The cab pulled up to the curb. It was Hakim again. "Taxi's here," Laura said.

"See you in class," called Ms. Greer.

Laura walked outside and then down the driveway. She climbed into the back of the cab. It would feel so good to get into bed.

Hakim turned the cab around and stopped at the corner. "Which way?" he asked.

Laura hesitated. She thought about all that filth in the Witlaw house.

"Please," said Hakim. "It's been a long and crazy night. Tell me where you want to go."

"I'm staying," she said. She got out of the cab and handed Hakim a five-dollar bill, to make up for the lost fare.

Hakim grinned at the easy money, then he grinned at Laura.

"You made a good choice," he laughed as he drove away. Laura watched the cab go, then she turned and walked back up the driveway.

She would begin with the laundry.

The Cactus People

"We'll have to spray you down when you get home," Pascal's mother said, glaring at him through the rearview mirror. "Don't come in the house until we delouse you."

"Turn the hose on him." Santora, his little sister, giggled. "Wash him like a dog."

"Pascal! Did you hear me? Take those things out of your ears when I talk to you."

"I don't have to go," Pascal said, kicking at the back of his sister's seat. "You could send a note. They're not going to argue with you."

"Don't start," his mother said. "There's no point in sending you to an expensive cathedral school if we don't follow the program. *You* fooled around; *you* created that mess for the caretaker; so *you* do the detention. And stop kicking the seat!"

Pascal slumped down, frowning as he watched the city of Cochabamba pass by his window. He hoped he was wrinkling his school uniform. No one should have to wear a school uniform on a Saturday. He pulled at his tie.

"I should have worn jeans," he said.

"Father Dominic probably wants you in uniform to inspire others," his mother said. "All those homeless people will see how sharp you look, and they'll pull up their socks and quit being such a fungus on Bolivian society. Like these people—look at them! Animals!"

They were stopped in traffic on a bridge. The riverbank was crowded with shanties and filthy people who were picking through garbage.

"Don't let any of them touch you," Pascal's mother said. "I don't even want to think about all the diseases they're carrying. I don't see why the priests are allowing them into the cathedral. The fumigating alone will cripple the maintenance budget." Pascal's mother served on several cathedral committees. It was one of the reasons Pascal was accepted into the cathedral school. That, and his ability with a soccer ball.

The traffic moved, but slowly. Instead of turning down the street that led to St. Anita's, his mother pulled the car over to the side of the road. "I'm letting you out here, Pascal. I don't want to keep battling with this traffic—your sister will be late for her riding lesson."

"Here? But I'm in my uniform!"

"Pascal, get out of the car. No one is paying any attention to you."

Pascal got out. Just as the car pulled away from the curb, his sister yelled out the window, "Look at that boy in a school uniform on a Saturday. He must be on detention!" He heard her laugh all the way down the road until the sound of it was swallowed up by traffic and other noise.

Pascal didn't look to see if anyone was staring. He broke into a run and kept it up for the six blocks to the cathedral. He arrived in the vestry, sweaty and panting.

"Ah, Pascal. There you are." Father Dominic had already arrived along with Marco from Pascal's class. "Splash some cold water on your face, then change into your cassock. You remember the service, I trust?"

"It was only last year," Pascal replied. Serving as an altar boy was compulsory at his school until age thirteen. Like most boys, Pascal had given it up the moment he could. Now fourteen, Pascal had plenty of other things to do with his time.

"Not so very long ago, then," said Father Dominic. "If you should forget anything, Marco here will remind you."

"You on detention, too?" Pascal whispered to Marco as he took his cassock off the cloakroom hook. "What did *you* do?"

"I chose to be here," Marco said, and Pascal made a face.

He saw Father Dominic packing up the communion things into a carrying bag.

"Why are you doing that?" Pascal asked. "Aren't we just going..." He motioned toward the door that led to the Cathedral's sanctuary.

"We're taking it on the road today," said Father Dominic. "Once a month we take Mass to the people on the Crown."

"The Crown?" No one lived on the Crown. "You mean the tourists?"

"You don't know anything, do you?" said Marco. "All that football and you don't know anything."

"Nothing wrong with sports," said Father Dominic, "and Pascal will know what we're talking about in a very short time. Ready? Off we go, then."

Just outside the vestry, in the courtyard of the church—which served as a playground for the school during the week—a group of people had gathered while Pascal had been changing. They carried boxes and baskets, and fell into line behind the priest and the altar boys. Now Pascal felt *very* conspicuous, walking down the busy Saturday streets in his cassock and surplice, carrying the giant crucifix, leading a sort of parade. They passed by street vendors: Indian women from the country, who walked into the city in their wide dirndl skirts and bowler hats, with babies slung on their backs, to sell their onions and carrots and coca leaves along the sidewalks. Shoppers, some crossing themselves, stood aside to let the procession pass by.

Pascal's iPod was in his trouser pocket. He wished he had the nerve to put in his earbuds and turn on some music. It would help him escape. But Father Dominic was sure to notice, and then there would be more detentions like this one.

"Ever been up on the Crown before?" Father Dominic was asking him. "On a school field trip, perhaps?"

"Once," Pascal replied. "Third grade. No, fourth grade." He'd teased a girl in his class and she'd retaliated by pouring Orange Fanta down his shirt. He remembered the stickiness and the flies more than he remembered the field trip.

"Nice healthy climb to the top," Father Dominic said.

"We're walking up?" But of course they were.

The people behind Pascal started singing a hymn. He tried to turn around to see how many had joined the procession, but twisting his body made the large crucifix waver and weave, and he faced front again.

They came out of the avenue and out onto the edge of the *Cancha*, the biggest market in Bolivia, which grew even bigger on Saturdays, spilling out onto roadsides and sidewalks. Pascal heard the merchants mumbling prayers as the procession passed by. He also heard the sounds of the amusement park at the bottom of San Sebastian Hill, which held the Crown. He wasn't allowed to go there. "Only lowlifes and troublemakers go to places like that" was one of his mother's proclamations. But Pascal and his friend Juan coordinated their stories one day and went there together. It had been fun, not at all like his mother had described it. It was families mostly, and guys holding hands with their girlfriends.

Pascal wished he were going to the amusement park today or, even better, to the bus station beyond the park where he could catch a bus that would take him all the way to Canada, where things were clean and cool—he'd seen pictures. Instead, he stayed next to Father Dominic, inhaling whiffs of incense from the burner Marco carried on the other side of the priest as they began the hike up the hill to the Crown.

The few tourists who were bothering with the monuments seemed surprised to see the religious procession. Some even took out their cameras and snapped pictures of them.

"I could hit them with the cross," Pascal said.

"What was that?" Father Dominic asked.

"Nothing, Father."

Finally, with his legs aching from the climb, Pascal was able to see the statue of *Las Heroinas*. It rose up at the end of the broad, tree-lined pathway and steps. Pascal hoped the father was in the mood for one of his short Masses. It would be a relief to ditch the cross and buy a soda.

"We turn this way now," said Father Dominic, steering him toward the trees.

"What? Where are we going?"

"To the Villa Miseria. Now, stay close."

Pascal wasn't likely to wander off, not here, as the procession moved through the stands of trees, down a path, and into a different world.

The stench hit Pascal almost before the sight did. It was like a scene out of a zombie movie, the hill baking out of the shade of the trees, everything dirt and dust and cactus and garbage.

A small crowd had gathered and more were appearing, stink rising from their rags and their skin, their eyes hollow, limbs thin and brittle-looking.

"I want to go," Pascal said.

"We will," said Father Dominic. "After Mass."

Pascal's cassock got caught on the thorns of a cactus bush. Father Dominic didn't notice and went on without him. Pascal began to panic.

"Wait! Wait!" he called out, even though Marco and the priest were just a few meters ahead, and the folks from the church were all around him. He started to let go of the cross to pull himself free, but the cross started to fall over, so he had to grab it again. The procession had their hands full already and began to step around him.

I'll be left here, Pascal thought. *The zombie-people will get me!*

Then, out of the cactus came a hand, slim with long fingers, which unhooked the cassock cloth from the cactus barbs. One of the fingers got pricked. Pascal saw a bright red drop of blood, then he was free and the hand was gone.

People bumped past him as he leaned down to see better—his curiosity, for the moment, greater than his fear.

The face that looked out at him was the most beautiful face he had ever seen. She was enchanting. She was more beautiful than any movie star or pop idol or those models in his mother's *Vogue*. For a long moment Pascal and the girl stared at each other, then the girl smiled, and Pascal thought he would melt into the dirt.

"*Gracias*," he whispered.

She whispered something back that he couldn't hear properly, or maybe it was in one of the Indian languages that he couldn't speak—all he knew was Spanish. He would have stayed like that all day long, stooped over and looking at the girl in the cactus bush, but Marco grabbed him and pulled him away.

"They are not zoo animals," Marco said. "They don't need to be stared at."

"I wasn't staring," protested Pascal, although how else could he explain what he was doing? He followed Marco to where Father Dominic had spread a clean white cloth over a portable table and was setting out the candles and the other altar objects. The procession was singing another hymn.

"What is this place?" Pascal asked Marco as they helped set up for Mass.

"It's where the *cleferos* live," Marco said. "Not all of them, of course. Some live down by the river. We go there sometimes, too. They live all over, really, except where we live." Marco's home was in the same section of Cochabamba as Pascal's, just a few streets over.

"*Cleferos?*"

"They breathe in the *clefa*, the glue. Open your eyes."

That was what Pascal had been smelling, or part of it. Many of the zombie-people clutched little plastic pots of glue which they held up to their noses. He saw a group of kids passing a pot around.

"They're our age!"

But Marco had moved on to help one of the people from the procession set up the fifteen Stations of the Cross, the paintings depicting Christ's last days, from his betrayal to his death and resurrection. Pascal glanced at the paintings leaning up against the rocks, looked away, then turned back to really see them. Jesus was depicted as a peasant, like any Bolivian from the country who worked the land. The Roman soldiers wore modern-day army uniforms. But it was still the Stations of the Cross, with the prayer in the garden, the kiss of betrayal, the arrest, and the flogging—it was all there.

"Let's begin," said Father Dominic.

The zombie-people—*cleferos*, Pascal corrected himself—were encouraged to gather around closer to the makeshift altar. The smell of unwashed clothes and bodies was almost too much.

But then he saw that face, the girl from the cactus bush. She had come out to take part in the Mass. All discomfort disappeared. Pascal held the cross straighter and squared his shoulders.

"Jesus was a *campesino*," Father Dominic began, and then the ritual of the Mass took over. Pascal was surprised that he remembered what to do.

People came forward to receive communion. Pascal

stood close to the priest. Father Dominic took a moment with each one, blessed them, spoke to them. Pascal began to distinguish faces. Some people cried. Some smiled. The boys who had been sharing the glue pot came up together, one of them still holding onto the little pot of *clefa*. Pascal wondered if they liked football.

After the Mass was cleared away, the table was spread with the food the people from the church had carried up the hill with them. Pascal was recruited to scoop rice and wave flies away.

The peace of the Mass disappeared in the noise of people happy to be eating. Pascal kept looking for the girl from the cactus, hoping to talk to her again, but he didn't see her. He was hot from the sun and the weight of his surplice, and nauseated from the smell of food mixed with the stench that came with the lack of toilets and showers.

"Why don't they get jobs?" he heard his mother's voice say in his head. "Why don't the police do something? Why are people like that allowed to have children? They're worse than animals."

Pascal had had enough. He handed his ladle over to the man beside him and backed away from the table. He needed to escape from all this for a while. He found a large rock and climbed up it, hoping that a bit of a breeze might catch him and blow the stink away. From his perch, he could see a whole village of cactus bushes covered over by blue plastic tarps and opened-up garbage bags. He saw people duck into and crawl out of the tarp-covered cactus houses. Some had glue pots. Some had babies.

The church people started up another hymn. To block it out, Pascal took his iPod out of his trouser pocket, put the earphones in his ears, and closed his eyes. Coldplay flooded his brain.

He felt a hand on his arm. He jumped and opened his eyes. The girl from the cactus bush was beside him. She said something he couldn't understand, but he smiled at her anyway.

She pointed at his iPod, then to her own ears.

He reached up to take the buds out of his ears, but his hands stopped halfway up. What if she had some sort of disease? Could he get lice or germs from sharing his earphones with her?

The hesitation lasted only a few seconds, but that was enough for her to get the message. Her smile vanished, her face closed down, and she backed herself down the rock. She turned her back on him and walked away.

All Pascal wanted to do then was rip off his cassock and get down off that hill. He wanted to be back in his bedroom, where things smelled good and he could play his video games and drink lots of Coke with lots of ice and live the way people were meant to live. But there was a clean-up to do, the gathering of all the Mass objects and the meal things, and then there were the good-byes, with Father Dominic actually hugging these people, Marco right in there with him. It was ages before they headed up and out of Villa Miseria, through the trees to the wide steps and walkways down the Crown, and down and away from San Sebastian Hill. He didn't speak a word on the way back to the cathedral, and no one intruded on his thoughts.

In the vestry, Pascal dumped his cassock and surplice in the laundry pile and left the church without responding to Father Dominic's "Thank you." He kept his school uniform jacket in his hand (he could smell the *cleferos* on his shirt), hailed a taxi, and went home.

"Outside," his mother said as he opened the door. "I don't want whatever you're bringing with you coming into this house. I've worked too hard at teaching that maid how to clean. Dump your clothes in the shed. Conchita will wash them out there. She's bringing you delousing shampoo, too."

"How am I supposed to wash my hair in the shed?"

"Use the hose," his mother said. He could hear his sister laughing.

Conchita brought him the shampoo and clean clothes, and took away his uniform for cleaning. Pascal slathered the shampoo all over himself. It smelled terrible, but it was a strong medicinal smell, not the stink of earlier.

"I don't know what Father Dominic is thinking sometimes," his mother said at dinner. "Maybe he's one of those Communist priests the church was supposed to have gotten rid of. Honestly, does he really think he can save those animals? Do they even have souls?"

Pascal thought about the priest embracing people in Villa Miseria, not minding the filth and the smell. He thought about the cactus girl's face when he wouldn't share the iPod.

"It wasn't like that," he said.

"Wasn't like what?"

Pascal put his fork loaded with beef and potatoes back on his plate. His mother and sister had gotten their nails done after the riding lesson. They were holding their forks awkwardly, not wanting to chip the new, long, shiny additions sprouting at the end of their fingers. Conchita ran in and out of the kitchen with coffee and to get "the other kind of sugar." The house around them glistened and gleamed. Pascal opened his mouth to explain about the day, but his mother and sister were already off on another subject, mocking the clothes the others at the riding class had been wearing.

He left the table and went into his room. His video games, his DVDs, his books, even the Coke with lots of ice he yelled to Conchita to bring him—nothing made him feel the way it used to. The look on the cactus girl's face ruined everything.

∼◎

He got through Sunday by claiming homework and staying in his room. On Monday, he went to school early and grabbed Marco at his locker before class.

"I need to go back to the Crown," he said.

"We'll go next month."

"No. Today. And you need to come with me."

"Why?"

"Because I don't want to go by myself." The truth came out before Pascal could stop it.

"It's dangerous," Marco said. "We go as a group. It's dangerous to go alone. People have been robbed up there, even killed."

"So you're calling them criminals? I thought you were so charitable."

"Doesn't mean I'm stupid." Marco gathered his books for his first class and slammed his locker shut.

"They're poor, they're hungry, and they want money for *clefa*. I'm nobody to them."

"So you have to come with me, then. It's too dangerous for me to go alone."

"Then don't go." Marco walked away.

Pascal went out into the yard. The junior boys were playing football. One of the players missed a pass and the ball rolled by Pascal. He stopped it expertly with his foot and was about to kick it back when the bell rang. Some running, others dawdling, the kids made their way through the school doors.

Pascal acted then without thinking, as if the decision had already been made and he was just following orders. He picked up the soccer ball and walked out of the school yard. His iPod was in his pocket. He'd find the cactus girl and let her listen to his music; that would clear his conscience. The soccer ball had no purpose, but he felt better carrying it.

Before long he was back on the wide stone boulevard, climbing San Sebastian Hill toward the statue of the fighting women. Now that he was up here, he realized he didn't know how to find the pathway to Villa Miseria. The trees along the boulevard all looked the same. He tried to recall how far away the statue was when he had ducked through the trees with Father Dominic.

He found a footpath, but he didn't know if it was

the right footpath. Ahead of him were cactus bushes covered with tarps, but he couldn't be sure if they were the right bushes and the right tarps. He began looking inside. Faces peered out at him. Some of the people shrieked. Some lay on the ground and barely took notice.

"Ball," he heard someone say. "Ball."

A group of boys were walking behind him. Maybe it was the same group who had been sharing the glue pot yesterday. He couldn't say for sure.

He clutched the soccer ball closer to his chest. "Do you know a girl?" he asked in Spanish. He didn't know if they understood, so he tried to act it out, making wiggly movements down his head to mimic long hair. "A girl with long hair?"

One of the boys stepped closer and tried to take the ball. Pascal backed away. "Help me find the girl first, then I'll give you the ball."

There were more of them. Either they didn't understand him or they didn't care if he found the girl or not. He pulled the ball out of the reach of one boy, and it got popped out of his hands by another.

He let it go. The boys dribble-kicked the ball among the cactus huts, passing it back and forth with their bare feet. Pascal stood and watched, then turned to search for the girl again.

The ball hit him in the back.

"Hey!" He looked around see who'd thrown it. A boy bounced it from one foot to the other, then kicked it back over to Pascal. The boys watched Pascal—waited for him.

Pascal kicked the ball out and began running after it. For a little while they were just boys together, playing football.

Then he saw her—the cactus girl. He stopped in the middle of the play, letting the ball be captured.

She was sitting in the dirt outside a cactus hovel. There was garbage all around her. Pascal didn't notice the trash. He knelt down beside her, took out his iPod, and put the earbuds into her ears. Her fingers touched his as she adjusted the earpieces. He turned the music on, showing her the volume button. She smiled, closed her eyes, and started nodding her head to the music.

Pascal had only meant to show her the iPod, to let her use it for a little while, but now he decided to give it to her. He could always get another one. And he wanted to see the look on her face when she realized he was giving it to her to keep.

"It will be stolen," a voice beside him said. Father Dominic. "Or she'll sell it for *clefa*. Marco told me you'd come up here. You need to come back with me now."

He offered a hand and pulled Pascal to his feet.

The girl opened her eyes at the movement and gave him a smile. Pascal started to say something, but the girl closed her eyes again to listen to the music. Father Dominic led Pascal away.

∾

They were halfway down the hill before Pascal could speak.

"I don't know who I am," he said.

Father Dominic nodded. "That's a good place to begin."

A COMPANY
OF FOOLS

It is 1349 and the Plague is sweeping across Europe. Henri, an orphan living in St. Luc's Abbey in France, records the story of his friendship with Micah, a rough street boy who sings like an angel. Along with the choir, Micah and Henri are sent out of the abbey to sing and bring comfort to the people. But the Plague is coming to their very door, and neither Henri nor Micah, nor anyone else in their world, will ever be the same again.

"A perfect novel." —Deirdre Baker, *The Toronto Star*

"A powerful historical tale." —*Booklist*

- CLA Book of the Year Honour Book, 2003
- Geoffrey Bilson Award for Historical Fiction for Young People Honour Book, 2003
- Mr. Christie Silver Book Award, 2003
- Ruth & Sylvia Schwartz Award for Young Adult/Middle Reader Books shortlist, 2003
- Manitoba Young Readers' Choice Award shortlist, 2004
- Rocky Mountain Book Award shortlist, 2004

THE
HEAVEN
SHOP

Binti Phirim was once a child star of a popular radio program. Now she is scraping to survive. Both her parents have died of AIDS, and Binti struggles to keep her siblings together. Binti always believed she was special; now she is nothing but a common AIDS orphan. But even as she realizes there is no hope that their former life will be restored to them, Binti must find the strength to create a new life, a new family.

"A groundbreaking novel that should be in classroom libraries." —*Quill & Quire*

"By reading this gripping story, students will understand how the epidemic of AIDS in Africa has change individuals and whole societies." —*Kliatt*

"A poignant story." —*Booklist*

"Highly recommended." —*Resource Links*

"[Ellis] puts a compelling human face on an international social problem." —*VOYA*

- Golden Oak Award winner, 2006
- Jane Addams Children's Book Award Winner (Honor Books for Older Children), 2005
- Alberta Children's Choice Book Award shortlist, 2006
- Manitoba Young Readers' Choice Awards Honour Book, 2006
- Foreword Magazine Book of the Year Award finalist, 2004
- Children's Africana Book Awards Honor Book for Older Readers, 2005
- Canadian Children's Book Centre Our Choice selection, 2005
- Ruth & Sylvia Schwartz Children's Book Award for Young Adult/Middle Reader Books finalist, 2005
- Red Maple Award shortlist, 2005

JAKEMAN

Along with his sister, Jake has been visiting their mother in prison ever since she was arrested for possession and trafficking three years ago. Despite his inspired letter-writing campaign to the Governor, nothing has changed. Their mom is still in prison. But Jake, a budding comic-book artist, has an alter-ego named Jakeman, the Barbed-Wire Boy. And this visit is going to be different. This time, Jakeman has a plan, and he's taking charge.

"Remarkable."   —*Midwest Book Review*

"Ellis explores important, often uncomfortable, questions ...[Her] approach to this difficult topic is sensitive and age-appropriate. These are children society calls 'damaged,' but...readers won't soon forget them."
   —*School Library Journal*

"Ellis's generally light touch makes the characters relatable; unexpected plot twists keep the action moving; and the current of sadness running through the book is realistic."   —*Horn Book*

- Diamond Willow Award nominee, 2008
- Silver Birch shortlist, 2007
- CLA Children's Book of the Year Award shortlist, 2008
- VOYA's Top Shelf Fiction for Middle School Readers list, 2007
- Hackmatack Children's Choice Book Award nominee, 2008-2009
- CCBC's Best Books for Kids & Teens Starred Choice, 2008

and with Eric Walters

BIFOCAL

When a Muslim boy is arrested on suspicion of terrorist activity, the high-school population becomes polarized. Haroon, a Muslim, is a serious student devoted to his family. Jay is a rising football star, fiercely devoted to his team. Amid an atmosphere of growing racial tension, both boys set out on a painful journey of self-discovery, where they must question their loyalties and the beliefs they have always taken for granted.

"This is a story that will leave readers looking at their school and themselves with new eyes." —*Booklist*

"This thought-provoking novel works extremely well as an examination of the dangers of racism and the redeeming value of tolerance." —*Quill & Quire*

"A suspenseful story." —*Kliatt*

"Energetic and thoughtful...an excellent resource."
—*ForeWord Magazine*

- White Ravens' Outstanding New International Books for Children and Young Adults list, 2008
- ForeWord Magazine's Book of the Year Award Bronze Medal (YA Fiction category), 2007
- Snow Willow Award nominee, 2008
- CCBC's Best Books for Kids & Teens, 2008